Sir Arthur Helps

The Life of Columbus

The Discoverer of America

Sir Arthur Helps

The Life of Columbus
The Discoverer of America

ISBN/EAN: 9783337333713

Printed in Europe, USA, Canada, Australia, Japan

Cover: Foto ©Raphael Reischuk / pixelio.de

More available books at **www.hansebooks.com**

THE

LIFE OF COLUMBUS.

THE DISCOVERER OF

AMERICA.

CHIEFLY BY SIR ARTHUR HELPS, K.C.B.

AUTHOR OF " THE SPANISH CONQUEST IN AMERICA,"

" FRIENDS IN COUNCIL," ETC.

TENTH EDITION.

LONDON:

GEORGE BELL AND SONS, YORK STREET,

COVENT GARDEN.

1890..

TO

WILLIAM HENRY STONE,

THIS LIFE OF COLUMBUS

IS DEDICATED

WITH SINCERE ESTEEM AND REGARD

BY HIS AFFECTIONATE

FRIEND,

ARTHUR HELPS.

London, *October*, 1868.

PREFACE.

THIS Life of Columbus is one of a series of biographies prepared under my superintendence, and for the most part taken verbatim from my "History of the Spanish Conquest in America."

That work was written chiefly with a view to illustrate the history of slavery, and not to give full accounts of the deeds of the discoverers and conquerors of the New World, much less to give a condensed memoir of each of them.

It has, therefore, been necessary to re-arrange and add considerably to these materials, and for this assistance I am indebted to the skill and research of Mr. Herbert Preston Thomas.

Perhaps there are few of the great personages

in history who have been more talked about and written about than Christopher Columbus, the discoverer of America. It might seem, therefore, that there is very little that is new to be said about him. I do not think, however, that this is altogether the case. Absorbed in, and to a certain extent overcome by the contemplation of the principal event, we have sometimes, perhaps, been mistaken as to the causes which led to it. We are apt to look upon Columbus as a person who knew that there existed a great undiscovered continent, and who made his way directly to the discovery of that continent—springing at one bound from the known to the unknown. Whereas, the dream of Columbus's life was to make his way by an unknown route to what was known, or to what he considered to be known. He wished to find out an easy pathway to the territories of Kublai Khan, or Prester-John.

Neither were his motives such as have been generally supposed. They were, for the most part, purely religious. With the gold gained from potentates such as Kublai Khan, the Holy Sepulchre was to be rebuilt, and the Catholic

Faith was to be spread over the remotest parts of the earth.

Columbus had all the spirit of a crusader, and, at the same time, the investigating nature of a modern man of science. The Arabs have a proverb that a man is more the son of the age in which he lives than of his own father. This was not so with Columbus; he hardly seems to belong at all to his age. At a time when there was never more of worldliness and self-seeking; when Alexander Borgia was Pope; when Louis the Eleventh reigned in France, Henry the Seventh in England, and Ferdinand the Catholic in Arragon and Castille—about the three last men in the world to become crusaders—Columbus was penetrated with the ideas of the twelfth century, and would have been a worthy companion of Saint Louis in that pious king's crusade.

Again, at a time when Aristotle and " the Angelic Doctor " ruled the minds of men with an almost unexampled tyranny: when science was more dogmatic than theology; when it was thought a sufficient and satisfactory explanation to say that bodies falling to the earth descended because it is their nature to descend — Columbus regarded natural phenomena with the spirit of inductive philosophy that would belong to a follower of Lord Bacon.

Perhaps it will be found that a very great man seldom does belong to his period, as other men do to theirs. Machiavelli* says that the way to renovate states is always to go back to first principles, especially to the first principles upon which those states were founded. The same law, if law it be, may hold good as regards the renovation of any science, art, or mode of human action. The man who is too closely united in thought and feeling with his own age, is seldom the man inclined to go back to these first principles.

It is very noticeable in Columbus that he was a most dutiful, unswerving, and un-inquiring son of the Church. The same man who would have taken nothing for granted in scientific research, and would not have held himself bound by the authority of the greatest names in science, never

---

* Machiavelli was contemporary with Columbus. No two men could have been more dissimilar; and Machiavelli was thoroughly a product of his age, and a man who entirely belonged to it.

ventured for a moment to trust himself as a discoverer on the perilous sea of theological investigation.

In this respect Las Casas, though a churchman, was very different from Columbus. Such doctrines as that the Indians should be somewhat civilized before being converted, and that even baptism might be postponed to instruction,—doctrines that would have found a ready acceptance from the good bishop—would have met with small response from the soldierly theology of Columbus.

The whole life of Columbus shows how rarely men of the greatest insight and foresight, and also of the greatest perseverance, attain the exact ends they aim at. In this respect all such men partake the career of the alchemists, who did not transmute other metals into gold, but made valuable discoveries in chemistry. So, with Columbus. He did not rebuild the Holy Sepulchre; he did not lead a new crusade; he did not find his Kublai Khan, or his Prester John; but he brought into relation the New World and the Old.

It is impossible to read without the deepest

interest the account from day to day of his voyages.　It has always been a favourite speculation with historians, and, indeed, with all thinking men, to consider what would have happened from a slight change of circumstances in the course of things which led to great events.　This may be an idle and a useless speculation, but it is an inevitable one.　Never was there such a field for this kind of speculation as in the voyages, especially the first one, of Columbus.　The first point of land that he saw, and landed at, is as nearly as possible the central point of what must once have been the United Continent of North and South America. The least change of circumstance might have made an immense difference in the result.　The going to sleep of the helmsman, the unshipping of the rudder, (which did occur in the case of "The Pinzon,") the slightest mistake in taking an observation, might have made, and probably did make, considerable change in the event.　During that memorable first voyage of Columbus, the gentlest breeze carried with it the destinies of future empires.　Had he made his first discovery of land at a point much southward of that which he did discover, South America might have been colonized by the Spaniards with all the vigour that belonged to their first efforts at colonization; and, being a continent, might not afterwards have been so easily wrested from their sway by the maritime nations.

On the other hand, had some breeze, big with the fate of nations, carried Columbus northwards, it would hardly have been left for the English, more than a century afterwards, to found those Colonies which have proved to be the seeds of the greatest nation that the world is likely to behold.

It was, humanly speaking, singularly unfortunate for Spanish dominion in America, that the earliest discoveries of the Spaniards were those of the West India Islands. A multiplicity of governors introduced confusion, feebleness, and want of system, into colonial government. The numbers, comparatively few, of the original inhabitants in each island, were rapidly removed from the scene of action; and the Spaniards lacked, at the beginning, that compressing force which would have been found in the existence of a body of natives who could not have been re-

moved by the outrages of Spanish cruelty, the
strength of Spanish liquors, or the virulence of
Spanish diseases.*

The Monarchs of Spain, too, would have been
compelled to treat their new discoveries and conquests more seriously. To have held the country
at all, they must have held it well. It would not
have been Ovandos, Bobadillas, Nicuesas and
Ojedas who could have been employed to govern, discover, conquer, colonize—and ruin by
their folly—the Spanish possessions in the Indies.
The work of discovery and conquest, begun by
Columbus, must then have been entrusted to men
like Cortes, the Pizarros, Vasco Nuñez, or the
President Gasca; and a colony or a kingdom
founded by any of these men might well have
remained a great colony, or a great kingdom, to
the present day.

ARTHUR HELPS.

London, *October*, 1868.

---

* The small-pox, for instance, was a disease introduced
by the Spaniards, which the comparatively feeble constitution of the Indians could not withstand.

CONTENTS.

THE LIFE OF COLUMBUS.

CHAPTER I.

Early Discoveries in the Fifteenth Century.

ODERN familiarity with navigation renders it difficult for us to appreciate adequately the greatness of the enterprise which was undertaken by the discoverers of the New World. Seen by the light of science and of experience, the ocean, if it has some real terrors, has no imaginary ones. But it was quite otherwise in the fifteenth century. Geographical knowledge was but just awakening, after ages of slumber; and throughout those ages the wildest dreams had mingled fiction with fact. Legends telling of monsters of the deep, jealous of invasion of their territory; of rocks of loadstone, powerful enough to extract every particle of iron from a passing ship; of stagnant seas and fiery skies; of wandering saints and flying islands; all combined to invest the unknown with the terrors of the supernatural, and to deter the explorer of the great ocean. The half-decked vessels that crept along the Mediterranean shores were but ill-fitted to bear the brunt of the furious waves of the Atlantic. The now indispensable sextant was but clumsily anticipated by the newly invented astrolabe. The use of the compass had scarcely become familiar to navigators, who indeed but imperfectly understood its properties. And who could tell, it was objected, that a ship which might succeed in sailing down the waste of waters would ever be able to return, for would not the voyage home be a perpetual journey up a mountain of sea?

But the same tradition which set forth the difficulties of reaching the undiscovered countries promised a splendid reward to the successful voyager. Rivers rolling down golden sand, mountains shining with priceless gems, forests fragrant with rich spices were among the substantial advantages to be expected as the result of the enterprise. " Our quest there," said Peter Martyr, " is not for the vulgar products of Europe." The proverb *Omne ignotum pro magnifico* was abundantly illustrated. And there was another object, besides gain, which was predominant in the minds of almost all the early explorers, namely, the spread of the Christian religion. This desire of theirs, too, seems to have been thoroughly genuine and deep-seated ; and it may be doubted whether the discoveries would have been made at that period but for the impulse given to them by the most religious minds longing to promote, by all means in their power, the spread of what, to them, was the only true and saving faith. " I do not," says a candid historian* of that age, " imagine that I shall persuade the world that our intent was only to be preachers ; but on the other hand the world must not fancy that our intent was merely to be traders." There is much to blame in the conduct of the first discoverers in Africa and America ; it is, however, but just to acknowledge that the love of gold was by no means the only motive which urged them to such

---

* Faria y Sousa

endeavours as theirs. To appreciate justly the intensity of their anxiety for the conversion of the heathen, we must keep in our minds the views then universally entertained of the merits and efficacy of mere formal communion with the Church, and the fatal consequences of not being within that communion.

This will go a long way towards explaining the wonderful inconsistency, as it seems to us, of the most cruel and wicked men believing themselves to be good Christians and eminent promoters of the faith, if only they baptized, before they slew, their fellow-creatures. And the maintenance of such church principles will altogether account for the strange oversights which pure and high minds have made in the means of carrying out those principles, fascinated as they were by the brilliancy and magnitude of the main object they had in view.

But while piety, sometimes debased into religious fanaticism, had a large part in these undertakings, doubtless the love of adventure and the craving for novelty had their influence also. And what adventure it was! New trees, new men, new animals, new stars; nothing bounded, nothing trite, nothing which had the bloom taken off it by much previous description! The early voyagers, moreover, were like children coming out to take their first gaze into the world, with ready credulity and unlimited fancy, willing to believe in fairies and demons, Amazons and mystic islands, " forms of a lower hemisphere," and fountains of perpetual youth.

The known world, in the time of Prince Henry of Portugal (at whose discoveries it will be convenient to take a preliminary glance), was a very small one indeed. The first thing for us to do is to study our maps and charts. Without frequent reference to these, a narrative like the present forms in our mind only a mirage of names and dates and facts, is wrongly apprehended even while we are regarding it, and soon vanishes away. The map of the world being before us, let us reduce it to the proportions it filled in Prince Henry's time; let us look at our infant world. First take away those two continents, for so we may almost call them, each much larger than a Europe, to the far west. Then cancel that square massive-looking piece to the extreme south-east; its days of penal settlements and of golden fortunes are

yet to come.   Then turn to Africa; instead of
that form of inverted cone which it presents, and
which we now know there are physical reasons
for its presenting, make a scimetar shape of it, by
running a slightly curved line from Juba on the
eastern side to Cape Nam on the western.   De-
clare all below that line unknown.   Hitherto, we
have only been doing the work of destruction;
but now scatter emblems of hippogriffs and anthro-
pophagi on the outskirts of what is left on the
map, obeying a maxim, not confined to the ancient
geographers only: "Where you know nothing,
place terrors."   Looking at the map thus completed, we can hardly help thinking to ourselves,
with a smile, what a small space, comparatively
speaking, the known history of the world has
been transacted in, up to the last four hundred
years.   The idea of the universality of the Roman
dominion shrinks a little; and we begin to think
that Ovid might have escaped his tyrant.*   The

---

* But the empire of the Romans filled the world; and
when that empire fell into the hands of a single person, the
world became a safe and dreary prison for his enemies.
The slave of imperial despotism, whether he was condemned
to drag the gilded chain in Rome and his senate, or to wear

of the eastern world. It was here that the Portuguese first planted a firm foot in Africa; and the
date of this town's capture may, perhaps, be taken
as that from which Prince Henry began to meditate further and far greater conquests. His aims,
however, were directed to a point long beyond
the range of the mere conquering soldier. He
was especially learned, for that age of the world,
being skilled in mathematical and geographical
knowledge. He eagerly acquired from Moors of
Fez and Morocco, such scanty information as
could be gathered concerning the remote districts
of Africa. The shrewd conjectures of learned
men, the confused records of Arabic geographers,
the fables of chivalry, were not without their influence upon an enthusiastic mind. The especial
reason which impelled the prince to take the
burden of discovery on himself was that neither
mariner nor merchant would be likely to adopt
an enterprise in which there was no clear hope
of profit. It belonged, therefore, to great men
and princes; and amongst such, he knew of no
one but himself who was inclined to it. This is
not an uncommon motive. A man sees something that ought to be done, knows of no one that

will do it but himself, and so is driven to the
enterprise even should it be repugnant to him.

Prince Henry, then, having once the well-

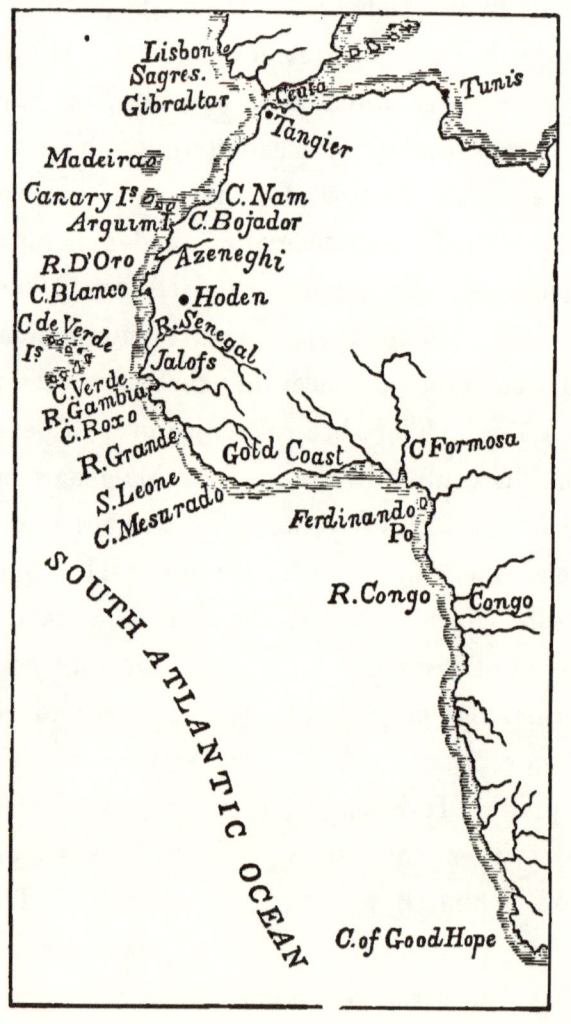

grounded idea in his mind that Africa did not end, according to the common belief, at Cape Nam,* but that there was a region beyond that forbidding negative, seems never to have rested until he had made known that quarter of the world to his own. He fixed his abode upon the promontory of Sagres, at the southern part of Portugal, whence, for many a year, he could watch for the rising specks of white sail bringing back his captains to tell him of new countries and new men.

One night, in the year 1418, he is thought to have had a dream of promise, for on the ensuing morning he suddenly ordered two vessels to be got ready forthwith, and placed them under the command of two gentlemen of his household, Zarco and Vaz, whom he directed to proceed down the Barbary coast on a voyage of discovery. A contemporary chronicler, Azurara, tells the story more simply, and merely states that these captains were young men, who, after the ending of the Ceuta campaign, were as eager for employment as the prince for discovery; and that they

---

* Portuguese for *Not*.

were ordered on a voyage having for its object the general molestation of the Moors as well as the prosecution of discoveries beyond Cape Nam.

The Portuguese mariners had a proverb about the Cape, " He who would pass Cape Not either will return or not," *Quem passar o Cabo de Nam, ou tornará ou nam,* intimating that if he did not turn before passing the Cape he would never return at all.   On this occasion it was not destined to be passed, for the two captains were driven out of their course by storms, and accidentally discovered a little island, where they took refuge, and which, from that circumstance, they called Porto Santo. On their return their master was delighted with the news they brought him, more on account of its promise than its substance.   In the same year he sent them out again with a third captain, Bartho-lomew Perestrelo, to convey a supply of seeds and animals for the newly-found island. Unfortunately, however, among the animals were some rabbits, which multiplied so rapidly that they overspread the whole island, and, by devouring every plant and blade of grass which grew there, soon changed a fruitful land into a bare wilderness.

In the following year, Zarco and Vaz, seeing

Porto Santo something that seemed like a
ıd, but yet different (the origin of so much
scovery, noting the difference in the likeness),
ouilt two boats, and, making for this cloud, soon
found themselves alongside a beautiful island
abounding in many things, but most of all in
trees, on which account they gave it the name
of Madeira (wood). The two discoverers landed
upon the island in different places. The prince,
their master, afterwards rewarded them with the
captaincies of the districts adjacent to those places.
To Perestrelo he gave the island of Porto Santo,
to colonize it. Perestrelo, however, did not make
much of his captaincy; and spent his life in endeavouring to make head against the rabbits, which
were as destructive as a plague of locusts, and
which by their fecundity resisted all his efforts to
exterminate them. This captain has a place in
history, as being the father-in-law of Columbus,
who, indeed, lived at Porto Santo for some time,
and here, on new found land, studied the cosmographical works which Perestrelo had been at
pains to accumulate; meditating far bolder discoveries.

Zarco and Vaz began the cultivation of their

island of Madeira, but met with an untoward event at first. In clearing the wood, they kindled a fire amongst it, which burned for seven years, we are told; and, in the end, that which had given its name to the island, and which, in the words of the historian, overshadowed the whole land, became the most deficient commodity. The captains founded churches in the island, and the King of Portugal, Don Duart, gave the temporalities to Prince Henry, and all the spiritualities to the Knights of Christ.

From this time forth, Prince Henry prosecuted his explorations with a fixity of purpose which could not but ensure success. Through every discouragement he persevered still. Many a Swiss peak has gone through three phases. It has been pronounced, first, " inaccessible," then, "a very dangerous ascent," and finally, "a pleasant excursion." So it was with each fresh headland which seemed to bar the way down the African coast. And the travellers who came last, in each case, found it next to impossible to imagine what were the difficulties and dangers that had seemed so formidable to their predecessors.

For a long time Cape Bojador, which is situate

seventy leagues to the south of Cape Nam, was the extreme limit of discovery. This cape was formidable in itself, being terminated by a ridge of rocks, with fierce currents running round them; but was much more formidable from the fancies which the mariners had formed of the sea and land beyond it. " It is clear," they were wont to say, " that beyond this cape there are no people whatever; the land is as bare as Libya— no water, no trees, no grass in it; the sea so shallow, that at a league from the land it is only a fathom deep; the currents so fierce, that the ship which passes that cape will never return;" and thus their theories were brought in to justify their fears.

This outstretcher (for such is the meaning of the word Bojador) was therefore as a bar drawn across that advance in maritime discovery, which had for so long a time been the first object of Prince Henry's life.

For twelve years the prince had been sending forth ships and men, with little approbation from the public—the discovery of Madeira and Porto Santo serving to whet his appetite for further enterprise, but not winning the common voice in

favour of his projects.   The people at home, im-
proving upon the reports of the sailors, said that
" the land which the prince sought after was
merely some sandy place like the deserts of
Libya; that princes had possessed the empire
of the world, and yet had not undertaken such
designs as his, nor shown such anxiety to find
new kingdoms; that the men who arrived in those
foreign parts (if they did arrive) turned from white
into black men; that the king, Don John, the
prince's father, had endowed foreigners with land
in his kingdom, to break it up and cultivate it,—
a thing very different from taking the people out
of Portugal, which had need of them, to bring
them amongst savages to be eaten, and to place
them upon lands of which the mother country had
no need; that the Author of the world had provided these islands solely for the habitation of
wild beasts, of which an additional proof was that
those rabbits which the discoverers themselves
had introduced were now dispossessing them of
the island."

There is much here of the usual captiousness
to be found in the criticism of bystanders upon
action, mixed with a great deal of false assertion

and assumed knowledge of the ways of Providence. Still, it were to be wished that most criticism upon action was as wise; for that part of the common talk which spoke of keeping their own population to bring out their own resources, had a wisdom in it which the men of future centuries were yet to discover throughout the Peninsula.

Prince Henry, as may be seen by his perseverance up to this time, was not a man to have his purposes diverted by such criticism, much of which must have been, in his eyes, worthless and inconsequent in the extreme. Nevertheless, he had his own misgivings. His captains came back one after another, with no good tidings of discovery, but with petty plunder gained as they returned from incursions on the Moorish coast. The prince concealed from them his chagrin at the fruitless nature of their attempts, but probably did not feel it less on that account. He began to think, Was it for him to hope to discover that land which had been hidden from so many princes? Still he felt within himself the incitement of " a virtuous obstinacy," which would not let him rest. Would it not, he thought, be ingratitude to God, who thus moved his mind to

C

these attempts, if he were to desist from his work,
or be negligent in it ?   He resolved, therefore, to
send out again Gil Eannes, one of his household,
who had been sent the year before, but had returned, like the rest, having discovered nothing.
He had been driven to the Canary Islands, and
had seized upon some of the natives there, whom
he brought back.   With this transaction the prince
had shown himself dissatisfied; and Gil Eannes,
now entrusted again with command, resolved to
meet all dangers, rather than to disappoint the
wishes of his master.   Before his departure, the
prince called him aside and said, " You cannot
meet with such peril that the hope of your reward shall not be much greater; and, in truth, I
wonder what imagination this is that you have all
taken up—in a matter, too, of so little certainty;
for if these things which are reported had any
authority, however little, I would not blame you
so much.   But you quote to me the opinions of
four mariners, who, as they were driven out of
their way to Frandes or to some other ports to
which they commonly navigated, had not, and
could not have used, the needle and the chart:
but do you go, however, and make your voyage

without regard to their opinion, and, by the grace of God, you will not bring out of it anything but honour and profit."

We may well imagine that these stirring words of the prince must have confirmed Gil Eannes in his resolve to efface the stain of his former mis-adventure. And he succeeded in doing so; for he passed the dreaded Cape Bojador—a great event in the history of African discovery, and one that in that day was considered equal to a labour of Hercules. Gil Eannes returned to a grateful and most delighted master. He informed the prince that he had landed, and that the soil ap-peared to him unworked and fruitful; and, like a prudent man, he could not only tell of foreign plants, but had brought some of them home with him in a barrel of the new-found earth, plants much like those which bear, in Portugal, the roses of Santa Maria. The prince rejoiced to see them, and gave thanks to God, " as if they had been the fruit and sign of the promised land; and besought our Lady, whose name the plants bore, that she would guide and set forth the doings in this discovery to the praise and glory of God, and to the increase of His holy faith."

The old world had now obtained a glimpse
beyond Cape Bojador. The fearful "outstretcher"
had no longer much interest for them, being a thing
that was overcome, and which was to descend from
an impossibility to a landmark, from which, by
degrees, they would almost silently steal down the
coast, counting their miles by thousands, until
Vasco de Gama should boldly carry them round
to India. But now came stormy times for the
Portuguese kingdom, and the troubles of the
regency occupied the prince's attention to the
exclusion of cosmography.

In 1441, however, there was a voyage which
led to very important consequences. In that
year Antonio Gonçalvez, master of the robes to
Prince Henry, was sent out with a vessel to load
it with skins of "sea-wolves," a number of them
having been seen, during a former voyage, at the
mouth of a river about a hundred and fifty miles
beyond Cape Bojador. Gonçalvez resolved to sig-
nalize his voyage by a feat that should gratify his
master more than the capture of sea-wolves; and
he accordingly planned and executed successfully
an expedition for seizing some Azeneghi Moors,
in order, as he told his companions, to take home

"some of the language of that country." Tris-
tam, another of Prince Henry's captains, afterwards falling in with Gonçalvez, a further capture
of Moors was made, and Gonçalvez returned to
Portugal with the spoil. This voyage seems to
have prompted the application which Prince Henry
made, in the same year, to Pope Martin the Fifth,
praying that his holiness would grant to the Portuguese crown all that should be conquered, from
Cape Bojador to the Indies, together with plenary
indulgence for those who should die while engaged
in such conquests. The pope granted these requests; though afterwards, as we shall see, the
Spanish discoveries of Columbus and his successors
rendered it necessary that the terms of the grant
should be modified. "And now," says a Portuguese historian, "with this apostolic grace, with
the breath of royal favour, and already with the
applause of the people, the prince pursued his
purpose with more courage, and with greater
outlay."

One proof of this popular approval was furnished by the formation of a company at Lagos,
in 1444, who received permission from the prince
to undertake discovery along the coast of Africa,

paying him a certain portion of any gains which they might make. Whether the company was expressly founded for slave traffic may be doubtful; but it is certain that this branch of their business was soon found to be the most lucrative one, and that from this time Europe may be said to have made a distinct beginning in the slave-trade, henceforth to spread on all sides, like the waves on troubled water, and not, like them, to become fainter and fainter as the circles widen. For slavery was now assuming an entirely new phase. Hitherto, the slave had been merely the captive in war, " the fruit of the spear," as he has figuratively been called, who lived in the house of his conqueror, and laboured at his lands. Now, however, the slave was no longer an accident of war. He had become the object of war. He was no longer a mere accidental subject of barter. He was to be sought for, to be hunted out, to be produced; and this change accordingly gave rise to a new branch of commerce.

Some time before 1454 a Portuguese factory was established at one of the Arguim islands, and this factory soon systematized the slave-trade. Thither came all kinds of merchandize from Portugal, and gold and slaves were taken back in return; the number of the latter sent home annually, at the time of Ca da Mosto's visit in 1454, being between seven and eight hundred.

The narrative of the Portuguese voyages along the African coast is, for the most part, rather uninviting. It abounds with names, and dates, and facts; but the names are often hard to pronounce, the dates have sometimes an air of uncertainty about them, and the facts stand out in hard relief, dry and unattractive. Could we recall, however, the voyagers themselves, and listen to their story, we should find it animating enough. Each enterprise, as we have it now, with its bare statistics, seems a meagre affair; but it was far otherwise to the men who were concerned in it. Of the motives* impelling men to engage in such expe-

---

* " They err who regard the conquistadores as led only by a thirst for gold, or even exclusively by religious fanaticism. Dangers always exalt the poetry of life, and moreover, the powerful age which we here seek to depict in regard to its influence on the development of cosmical ideas, gave to all enterprises, as well as to the impressions of nature offered by distant voyages, the charm of novelty

ditions, something has already been said. But besides the hopes and fears of each individual of the crew, the conjoint enterprise had in it a life to be lived, and a career to be worked out. It started to do something; fulfilled its purpose, or at least some purpose; and then came back, radiant with success—from that time forward to be a great fact in history. Or, on the other hand, there was some small failure or mischance, perhaps early in the voyage; the sailors then began to reckon up ill omens, and to say that little good would come of this business. Further on, some serious misadventure happened which made them turn, or from the mere lapse of time they were obliged to bethink themselves of getting back. Safety, not renown or profit, now became their object; and then hope was at last but the negative of some fear. Thereupon, no doubt, ensued a good deal of recrimination amongst themselves, for very few people are magnanimous enough to

---

and surprise, which begins to be wanting to our present more learned age in the many regions of the earth which are now open to us."—HUMBOLDT's *Kosmos.* Sabine's translation, 1848, vol. ii. p. 272.

share ill-success kindly together. Then, in the long dull evenings of their voyage homewards, as they sat looking on the waters, they thought what excuses and explanations they would make to their friends at home, and how shame and vexation would mingle with their joy at returning.

This transaction, teeming, as it did, with anxious life, makes but a poor show in some chronicle :— they sailed, and did something, or failed in doing, and then came back, and this was in such a year : —brief records, like the entry in an almanack, or the few emphatic words on a tombstone.

At the period, however, we are now entering upon, the annals of maritime discovery are fortunately enriched by the account of a voyager who could tell more of the details of what he saw than we have hitherto heard from other voyagers, and who was himself his own chronicler.

In 1454, Ca da Mosto, a young Venetian, who had already gained some experience in voyaging, happened to be on board a Venetian galley that was detained by contrary winds at Cape St. Vincent. Prince Henry was then living close to the Cape. He sent his secretary and the Venetian consul on board the galley. They told of the

great things the prince had done, showed samples
of the commodities that came from the lands discovered by him (Madeira sugars, dragon's blood,
and other articles), and spoke of the gains made
by Portuguese voyagers being as great as 700 or
1000 per cent. Ca da Mosto expressed his wish
to be employed, was informed of the terms that
would be granted, and heard that a Venetian
would be well received by the prince, " because
he was of opinion, that spices and other rich
merchandise might be found in those parts, and
knew that the Venetians understood these commodities better than any other nation."

In fine, Ca da Mosto saw the prince, and was
evidently much impressed by his noble bearing.
He obtained his wishes, and being furnished with
a caravel, he embarked his merchandise in it, and
set off on a voyage of discovery. There was now,
for the first time, an intelligent man on board one
of these vessels, giving us his own account of the
voyage.

From Ca da Mosto the reader at once learns
the state of things with regard to the slave-trade.
The Portuguese factory at Arguim was the head
quarters of the trade. Thither came all kinds

of merchandise; and gold and slaves were taken back in return. The "Arabs" of that district (Moors, the Portuguese would have called them) were the middle men in this affair. They took their Barbary horses to the negro country, and "there bartered with the great men for slaves," getting from ten to eighteen slaves for each horse. They also brought silks of Granada and Tunis, and silver, in exchange for which they received slaves and gold. These Arabs, or Moors, had a place of trade of their own, called Hoden, behind Cape Blanco. There the slaves were brought, "from whence," Ca da Mosto says, "they are sent to the mountains of Barka, and from thence to Sicily; part of them are also brought to Tunis, and along the coast of Barbary, and the rest to Argin, and sold to the licensed Portuguese. Every year between seven and eight hundred slaves are sent from Argin to Portugal."

"Before this trade was settled," says Ca da Mosto, "the Portuguese used to seize upon the Moors themselves (as appears occasionally from the evidence that has before been referred to), and also the Azenegues, who live further towards the south; but now peace is restored to all, and

the Infante suffers no further damage to be done
to these people. He is in hopes, that by con-
versing with Christians, they may easily be brought
over to the Romish faith, as they are not, as yet,
well established in that of Mohammed, of which
they know nothing but by hear-say."

No doubt the prince's good intentions were
greatly furthered by the convenience of this mode
of trading. In short, gain made for itself its usual
convenient channels to work in, and saved itself
as much as it could the trouble of discovery, or
of marauding. Ca da Mosto being, as was said
before, the first modern European visiting Africa
who himself gives an account of it, and being,
moreover, an honest and intelligent man, possess-
ing the rare combination of keen observation and
clear narrative power, all that he writes is most
valuable. He notices the differences, both as regards the people and the country, to be found
on the opposite sides of the Senegal River. On
the northern side he finds the men small, spare
and tawny, the country arid and barren; on the
southern side, the men " exceeding black, tall,
corpulent and well made; the country green, and
full of green trees." This latter is the country

of Jalof, the same that Prince Henry first heard of in his intercourse with the Moors. Both men and women, Ca da Mosto says, wash themselves four or five times a day, being very cleanly as to their persons, but not so in eating, in which they observe no rule. They are full of words, and never have done talking; and are, for the most part, liars and cheats. Yet, on the other hand, they are very charitable; for they give a dinner or a night's lodging and a supper, to all strangers who come to their houses, without expecting any return.

Leaving the country of the Jalofs, Ca da Mosto proceeded eight hundred miles further, as he says, (but he must, I think, have over-estimated his reckoning,) to the country of a negro potentate, called King Budomel. Here it appears that the religion, of the court at least, was Mohammedan, and Ca da Mosto records a conversation which he had with Budomel upon the subject. " The king asked him to give his opinion of their manner of worship, and also some account of his own religion. Hereupon Ca da Mosto told him, in presence of his doctors, that the religion of Mohammed was false, and the Romish the true

one. This made the Arabs mad, and Budomel
laugh; who, on this occasion, said that he looked
upon the religion of the Europeans to be good,
for that none but God could have given them so
much riches and understanding. He added, however, that the Mohammedan law must be also
good; and that he believed the negroes were
more sure of salvation than the Christians; because God was a just Lord, and therefore, as He
had given the latter Paradise in this world, it
ought to be possessed in the world to come by
the negroes, who had scarcely anything here, in
comparison with the others."

From Budomel's country the voyagers, sailing
southwards, came to the river Gambra (now called
Gambia), which they entered, but could not succeed in conciliating the natives, who attacked
them with signal valour, and maintained the contest with almost unparalleled bravery, considering
that the arms used by the Europeans were totally
unknown to their opponents.

During their stay in this river Ca da Mosto
and his companions saw the constellation of the
southern cross for the first time. Finding that
the natives would have nothing to do with them,

for they believed that the Christians were very bad people, and bought negroes to eat them, Ca da Mosto and the other commanders wished to proceed a hundred miles further up the river; but the common sailors would not hear of it, and the expedition forthwith returned to Portugal.

Two years later, in 1456, Ca da Mosto made another voyage, in the course of which he discovered the Cape de Verde Islands. Leaving them, he went again to the Gambia River, which he ascended much further than he had done during his previous expedition, and he also succeeded on this occasion in conciliating the natives. Then he went down the coast, passed Cape Roxo, and afterwards sailed up the Rio Grande, but, from want of any knowledge of the language of the people, was unable to prosecute his explorations among them.

Some time between 1460 and 1464, an expedition went out under Pedro de Cintra, one of the King of Portugal's gentlemen, to make further discoveries along the African coast. These voyagers, whose story is briefly told by Ca da Mosto, discovered Sierra Leone (so called on account of the roaring thunder heard there), and went a little beyond Cape Mesurado. The precise date of this voyage is uncertain, but we may fairly consider Sierra Leone as being the point attained at, or about, the death of Prince Henry in 1463, of whose character, before parting with him, something deserves to be said.

This great leader of maritime discovery resembled Columbus strongly in one thing, namely, his unity of purpose. He resembled him, too, in his patience and in his unvarying confidence of success, even under disappointment. " He was bold and valorous in war, versed in arts and letters; a skilful fencer; in the mathematics superior to all men of his time; generous in the extreme; most zealous for the increase of the faith. No bad habit was known in him. His memory was equal to the authority he bore, and his prudence equal to his memory."* And to this character the chronicler, Azurara, who evidently knew the prince well, and speaks with perfect honesty about him, adds two or three of those little niceties of description which give life and reality to the picture. He says that the prince

---

* Faria y Sousa.

was a man of great counsel and authority, wise and of good memory, but in some things slow, whether it was through the prevalence of the phlegmatic temperament in his constitution, or from intentional deliberation, being moved to some end which men did not perceive.

It was this temperament, probably, that made the prince incapable of " ill-will against any person, however great the injury he had received from him," so that this placidity of disposition seemed an actual fault in him. He was accordingly thought " deficient in distributive justice." There are instances in his conduct which bear out this, and one especially, in which he is stated to have overlooked the desertion of his banner, on an occasion of great peril to himself, and afterwards to have unjustly favoured the persons who had thus been found wanting in courage. This, no doubt, was an error on his part, but at least it was an heroic one, such as belonged to the first Cæsar; and in the estimation of the prince's followers, it probably added to their liking for the man what little it may have taken away from their confidence in the precision of his justice as a commander.

D

We learn, from the same authority, that his
house was the resort of all the good men of the
kingdom, and of foreigners, and that he was a
man of intense labour and study. " Often the
sun found him in the same place where it had
left him the day before, he having watched
throughout the whole arc of the night without
any rest."

Altogether, whether we consider this prince's
motives, his objects, his deeds, or his mode of life,
we must acknowledge him to be one of the most
notable men, not merely of his own country and
period, but of modern times and of all nations,
and one upon whose shoulders might worthily
rest the arduous beginnings of continuous maritime discovery. Would that such men remained
to govern the lands they have the courageous
foresight to discover! Then, indeed, they might
take to themselves the motto *talant de bien faire,*
which this prince, their great leader, caused to be
inscribed by his captains in many a land, that
as yet, at least, has not found much good from its
introduction, under his auspices, to the civilization
of an older world.

Hurrying over this preliminary sketch, we may

briefly note that about six years after Prince
Henry's death, the Gold Coast was explored by
Fernando Gomez, and the Portuguese fort was
built there which Columbus afterwards visited;
that Fernando Po discovered an island which was
then called Formosa, but which is now known by
the name of its discoverer; and that Diego Cam, accompanied, it is said, by Martin Behaim (Martin of
Bohemia), the most celebrated geographer of those
times—to whom, by the way, some of the credit
exclusively due to Columbus has been rather un-
fairly given—discovered the kingdom of Congo.
About this time an ambassador sent to the King
of Portugal by the sovereign of Benin, a territory
between the Gold Coast and Congo, happened to
speak about a greater power in Africa than his
master, to whom indeed his master was but the
vassal.   This instantly set the Portuguese king
thinking about Prester John, of whom legends
spoke as a Christian king ruling over a Christian
nation somewhere in what was vaguely called
the Indies; and the search after whom is, in
maritime discovery, what the alchemist's pursuit after the philosopher's stone was in chemistry.   The king concluded that this " greater

power" must be Prester John; and accordingly
Bartholomew Diaz and two other captains were
sent out on further discovery. They did not
find Prester John, but made their way southwards
along a thousand and fifty miles of new coast, as
far as a cape which, from experience, they called
Cape Stormy, but which their master, seeing in
its discovery an omen of better things, renamed
as the Cape of Good Hope.

It is a fact of great historical interest, and a
singular link between African and American discovery, that Bartholomew Columbus, brother of
Christopher, was engaged in this voyage. The
authority for this important statement is Las
Casas, who says that he found, in a book belonging to Christopher Columbus, being one of
the works of Cardinal Aliaco, a note " in Bartholomew Colon's handwriting," (which he knew
well, having several of the letters and papers
concerning the expedition in his own possession), which note gives a short account, in bad
Latin, of the voyage, mentions the degree of
latitude of the Cape, and concludes with the
words " *in quibus omnibus interfui.*"

In fiction, too, this voyage of Bartholomew

Diaz was very notable, as it presented an occasion for the writing of one of the most celebrated passages in modern poetry, a passage not easily to be surpassed for its majesty and tenderness, and for a beauty which even those tiresome allusions to the classics, that give a faded air to so much of the poetry of the sixteenth century, cannot seriously disfigure nor obscure.

It is to be found in the Lusiadas of Camöens, and indicates the culminating point of Portuguese discovery in Africa, as celebrated by the national poet.

Just as the mariners approach the Cape, a cloud rises, darkens the air, and then discloses a monstrous giant, with deep-set, caverned eyes, of rugged countenance, and pallid earthy colour, vast as that statue of Apollo, the colossal wonder of the world. In solemn language, this awful shape pours forth disastrous prophecies, and threatens his highest vengeance on those who have discovered him—maledictions which, alas! may be securely uttered against those who accomplish aught that is bolder than has hitherto been attempted by their fellow men.

When vexed by the question " Who art thou?"

the "stupendous body" harshly and mournfully replies, that he is that great stormy Cape, hitherto hidden from mankind, whom their boldness in discovering much offends.

He then relates the touching story of his love: how he was Adamastor, of the race of Titans, and how he loved Thetis, the fairest being of the sea; and how, deceived by the (magic) arts of her "who was the life of his body," he found himself caressing a rough and horrid crag instead of her sweet, soft countenance; and how, crazed by grief and by dishonour, he wandered forth to seek another world, where no one should behold him and mock his misery; how still the vengeance of the gods pursued him; and how he felt his flesh gradually turning into rock, and his members extending themselves among the long waves; and how, for ever to increase his agony, the beautiful Thetis still encircled him.

Having told his grief, he made himself into a dark cloud (*Desfez-se a nuvem negra*), and the sea roared far off with a sonorous sound. And then the Portuguese mariner lifted up his hands in prayer to the sacred chorus of angels, who had guided the vessel so long on its way, and prayed

God to remove the fulfilment of the evil things which Adamastor had prophesied against his nation.

The Genius of the Stormy Cape might have taken up a direr song of prophecy against the inhabitants of the unfortunate land of which he formed so conspicuous and mournful a prominence.

Maritime discovery had now, by slow and painful degrees, proceeded down the coast of Africa, nearly to the southernmost point, and from thence will soon be curving round in due course to India. But expeditions by sea were not the only modes of discovery undertaken by the Portuguese in the reign of John the Second of Portugal. Pedro de Covilham and Alfonso de Paiva went on an enterprise of discovery mainly by land. The latter died at Cairo, the former made his way to Cananor, Calecut, and Goa, and thence back to Cairo, where he found that his companion had died. He then set out again, and eventually came into the kingdom of Shoa,* to the court of

---

* A country in the south of Abyssinia. Tegulet, the ancient capital of Shoa, is in 38° 40′ E. long., and 9° 45′ N. lat.

"the King of Habbesh," who fulfilled sufficiently
in Covilham's eyes, the idea of Prester John, and
was accordingly called so. It is a curious coin-
cidence, that an ambassador from the King of
Habbesh, called Lucas Marcos, a priest of that
country, came about this time to Rome, and afterwards to Lisbon, which circumstance gave a new
impetus to all the King of Portugal's "hopes,
wishes, and endeavours."

A more remarkable person even than an ambassador from Prester John arrived nearly at the
same time at Lisbon. This was Bemoin, Prince
of Jalof. Bemoin came to seek the protection of
the King of Portugal, and the reason of his
coming was as follows. He was the brother,
on the mother's side, of Brian, King of Jalof.
This king was inert and vicious. He had,
however, the wisdom to make Bemoin prime
minister, and to throw all the cares and troubles
of governing upon him. Nothing was heard in
the kingdom but of Bemoin. But he, seeing,
perhaps, the insecurity of his position, diligently
made friends with the Portuguese, keeping aloof,
however, from becoming a convert, though he
listened respectfully to those who expounded the

Christian faith to him. Cibitab, a brother of the inert Brian, by the father's side, became jealous of Bemoin, revolted, killed Brian, and vanquished Bemoin, who thereupon threw himself upon the protection of his Portuguese friends, and came to Lisbon.

Bemoin was received magnificently by King John of Portugal. The negro prince had formerly alleged that one of his reasons for not becoming a Christian was the fear of disgusting his followers; but, being in Portugal, that reason no longer held good, and he became a convert, being baptized as Don John Bemoin, having King John for a godfather. Twenty-four of Bemoin's gentlemen received baptism after him. This is the account of his reception. "Bemoin, because he was a man of large size and fine presence, about forty years old, with a long and well-arranged beard, appeared indeed not like a barbarous pagan, but as one of our own princes, to whom all honour and reverence were due. With equal majesty and gravity of demeanour he commenced and finished his oration, using such inducements to make men bewail his sad fortune in exile, that only seeing these natural signs of sorrow, people

comprehended what the interpreter afterwards
said. Having finished the statement of his case
as a good orator would, in declaring that his only
remedy and only hope was in the greatness and
generosity of the king, with whom he spoke aside
for a short time, he was answered by the king in
few words, so much to his satisfaction that immediately it made a change in his whole look, spirits,
and bearing, rendering him most joyous. Taking
leave of the king, he went to kiss the queen's
hand, and then that of the prince, to whom he
said a few words, at the end of which he prayed
the prince that he would intercede in his favour
with the king.   And thence he was conducted
to his lodgings by all the nobility that had accompanied him."

After this, Bemoin had many conversations
with the king, and always acquitted himself well.
Amongst other things, he gave information respecting various African nations, and especially of
the king of a Jewish people, who in many things
resembled Christians.   Here again the Portuguese monarch was delighted at finding himself
upon the traces of Prester John.

It must not be forgotten to mention, that the

king made great rejoicings in honour of Bemoin's conversion, on which occasion the negro prince's attendants performed singular feats on horseback.

Bemoin maintained his favour at the Portuguese court, and succeeded in his object of obtaining military assistance. He was sent back to his own country with a Portuguese squadron of twenty caravels, which had for its instructions, besides his restitution, to found a fort on the banks of the river Senegal.

The Portuguese arrived at the river, and began building the fort, but are said to have chosen an unhealthy spot to build on. Whether they could have chosen a healthy one is doubtful. The commander, however, Pedro Vaz, thought that there was treachery on Bemoin's part, and killed him with the blow of a dagger on board his vessel. The building was discontinued, and Pedro Vaz returned to Portugal, where he found the king excessively vexed and displeased at the fate of Bemoin.

The historian may now stop in his task of tracing Portuguese discovery along the coast of Africa. We have seen it making its way with quiet perseverance, for seventy years, from Cape

Nam to the Cape of Good Hope, a distance of some six thousand miles. This long course of discovery has been almost entirely thrown into shade by the more daring and brilliant discovery of America, which we have now to enter upon. Yet these proceedings on the African coast had in them all the energy, perseverance, and courage which distinguished American discovery. Prince Henry himself was hardly a less personage than Columbus. They had different elements to contend in. But the man whom princely wealth and position, and the temptation to intrigue which there must have been in the then state of the Portuguese court, never induced to swerve from the one purpose which he maintained for forty years, unshaken by popular clamour, however sorely vexed he might be with inward doubts and misgivings; who passed laborious days and watchful nights in devotion to this one purpose, enduring the occasional short-comings of his agents with that forbearance which springs from a care for the enterprise in hand, so deep as to control private vexation (the very same motive which made Columbus bear so mildly with insult and contumely from his followers),—such a man is worthy to be put in comparison with the other great discoverer who worked out his enterprise through poverty, neglect, sore travail, and the vicissitudes of courts. Moreover, it must not be forgotten that Prince Henry was undoubtedly the father of modern geographical discovery, and that the result of his exertions must have given much impulse to Columbus, if it did not first move him to his great undertaking. After the above eulogium on Prince Henry, which is not the least more than he merited, his kinsmen, the contemporary Portuguese monarchs, should come in for their share of honourable mention, as they seem to have done their part in African discovery with much vigour, without jealousy of Prince Henry, and with high and noble aims. It would also be but just to include, in some part of this praise, the many brave captains who distinguished themselves in these enterprises.

How far the great discoverer, on whose career we are about to enter, was himself actually concerned in these African expeditions we have no means of deciding. But there can be little doubt that this raising the curtain of the unknown, this glimpse of new countries, gave a keen stimulus to the researches of geographers, and, in fact, set the fashion of discovery. Men's minds were drawn into this special channel; and it remained for Christopher Columbus first to form a sound theory out of the conflicting views of the cosmographers, and finally to carry out that theory with the boldness and resolution which have made his name one of those beacon-fires which carry on from period to period the tidings of the world's great history through successive ages.

CHAPTER II.

Early Years of Columbus.

THE question of Columbus's birthplace
has been almost as hotly contested as
that of Homer's. A succession of pam-
phleteers had discussed the pretensions of half a
dozen different Italian villages to be the birthplace of the great navigator; but still archæ-
ologists were divided on the subject, when, at
a comparatively recent period, the discovery
of the will in which Columbus bequeathed part
of his property to the Bank of Genoa, conclu-
sively settled the point in favour of that city.
"Thence I came," he says, "and there was I
born." As to the date of his birth there is no
such direct evidence; and conjectures and infer-
ences, founded on various statements in his own
writings, and in those of his contemporaries, range

over the twenty years from 1436 to 1456, in
attempting to assign the precise time of his appearance in the world. Mr. Irving adopts the
earlier of these two dates, upon the authority of
a remark by Bernaldez, the curate of Los Pala-
cios, which speaks of the death of Columbus in
the year 1506, "at a good old age, being seventy
years old, a little more or less." But this statement has an air of vagueness, and is, moreover,
inconsistent with several passages in Columbus's
own letters.* And the evidence of the ancient
authorities who seem most to be relied on, points
rather to the year 1447 or 1448 as the probable
date.

His father was a wool-carder; but this fact
does not necessarily imply, in a city of traders like
Genoa, that his family was of particularly humble
origin. At any rate, like most others, when the
light of a great man's birth is thrown upon its
records, real and possible, it presents some other
names not altogether unworthy to be inscribed

---

* "His hair," says his son Fernando, "turned white before he was thirty." This would add to his apparent age,
and might have deceived Bernaldez.

among the great man's ancestors. Christopher was not, he says in a letter to a lady of the Spanish court, the first admiral of his family—referring, evidently, to two naval commanders bearing his name, who had attained some distinction in the maritime service of Genoa and France, and the younger of whom, Colombo el Mozo, was in command of a French squadron in the expedition undertaken by John of Anjou against Naples for the recovery of the Neapolitan crown. But his relationship with these Colombos, if traceable at all, was probably only a very distant one, and his son, in admitting this, wisely says that the glory of Christopher is quite enough, without there being a necessity to borrow any from his ancestors.

At a very early age he became a student at the University of Pavia, where he laid the foundations of that knowledge of mathematics and natural science, which stood him in good stead throughout his life. At Genoa he would naturally regard the sea as the great field of enterprise which produced harvests of rich wares and spoils of glorious victories; and he may have heard, now and then, news of the latest conclusions of

E

the Arabic geographers at Senaar, and rumours of explorations down the African coast, which would be sure to excite interest among the maritime population of his birthplace. It is not wonderful that, exposed to such influences, he preferred a life of adventure on the sea to the drudgery of his father's trade in Genoa. Accordingly, after finishing his academical course at Pavia, he spent but a few irksome months as a carder of wool (*tector panni*) and actually entered on his nautical career before he was fifteen years old.

Of his many voyages, which of them took place before, and which after, his coming to Portugal, we have no distinct record; but are sure that he traversed a large part of the known world, that he visited England, that he made his way to Iceland and Friesland* (where he may possibly have

---

* The account of this voyage to the north of Europe, as commonly quoted, furnishes a singular instance of the inaccuracy of translators in the matter of figures. Columbus is there made to say, that at the Ultima Thule, which he reached, "the tides were so great as to rise and fall twenty-six fathoms," i. e. 156 feet. Of course this is an absurdity; for no tides in Europe rise much above fifty feet. We have no record of the exact words used by Columbus, but in the extant Italian translation he

heard vague tales of the discoveries by the North-
men in North America), that he had been at El
Mina, on the coast of Guinea, and that he had
seen the Islands of the Grecian Archipelago. " I
have been seeking out the secrets of nature for
forty years," he says, "and wherever ship has
sailed, there have I voyaged." But beyond a few
vague allusions of this kind, we know scarcely
anything of these early voyages. However, he
mentions particularly his having been employed
by King Réné of Provence to intercept a Venetian galliot. And this exploit furnishes illustra-
tions both of his boldness and his tact. During
the voyage the news was brought that the galliot
was convoyed by three other vessels. Thereupon
the crew were unwilling to hazard an engagement,
and insisted that Columbus should return to

---

is made to speak of the rise being *venti sei bracchia*, i.e.
twenty-six ells (not fathoms), or about fifty-two feet. But
even this reduced estimate must be excessive. Except
in the Bristol Channel there is no rise of tide in the seas of
Northern Europe which at all approaches this limit. At
Reikiavik (Iceland) the rise is seventeen and a half feet.
In Greenland it varies from a minimum of seven feet at
Julianshaab to a maximum of twelve and a half feet at
Frederikshaab.

Marseilles for re-inforcement. Columbus made a feint of acquiescence, but craftily arranged the compass so that it appeared that they were returning, while they were really steering their original course, and so arrived at Carthagena on the next morning, thinking all the while that they were in full sail for Marseilles.

Considering how much more real the hero of a biography appears if we can picture him accurately in our mind's eye, and see him " in his habit as he lived," it is singularly unfortunate that the personal appearance of Columbus has been so variously described by the old historians that it is impossible to speak with certainty on the subject. Strangely enough, too, no well-authenticated portrait of the great discoverer exists. Ferdinand Columbus, who would be a good authority, fails to give us, in describing his father, any of those little touches which make up a good literary photograph. We learn, however, that he had a commanding presence, that he was above the middle height, with a long countenance, rather full cheeks, an aquiline nose, and light grey eyes full of expression. His hair was naturally light in colour, but, as has been already stated, it turned nearly white while he was still a young man.

The peculiar characteristics of his mind are such as we might naturally expect to find in the originator of such a work as the discovery of America,—who was, indeed, one of the great spirits of the earth; but still of the same order of soul to which great inventors and discoverers have mostly belonged. Lower down, too, in mankind, there is much of the same nature leading to various kinds of worthy deeds, though there are no more continents for it to discover.

But to return to the renowned personage of whom we are speaking. There was great simplicity about him, and much loyalty and veneration. The truly great are apt to believe in the greatness of others, and so to be loyal in their relations here; while, for what is beyond here, a large measure of veneration belongs to them, as having a finer and more habitually present consciousness than most men of something infinitely above what even their imaginations can compass. He was as magnanimous as it was possible, perhaps, for so sensitive and impassioned a person to be. He was humane, self-denying, courteous. He had an intellect of that largely inquiring kind which may remind us of our great English philosopher, Bacon. He was singularly resolute and enduring. The Spaniards have a word, *longanimidad*, which has been well applied in describing him, as it signifies greatness and constancy of mind in adversity. He was rapt in his designs, having a ringing for ever in his ears of great projects, making him deaf to much, perhaps, that prudence might have heeded:—one to be loved by those near him, and likely by his presence to inspire favour and respect.

At what precise period his great idea came into his mind we have no means of ascertaining. The continuous current of Portuguese discoveries had, as we have seen, excited the mind of Europe, and must have greatly influenced Columbus, living in the midst of them. This may be said without in the least detracting from his merits as a discoverer. In real life people do not spring from something baseless to something substantial, as people in sick dreams. A great invention or discovery is often like a daring leap, but it is from land to land, not from nothing to something; and if we look at the subject with this consideration

fully before us, we shall probably admit that
Columbus had as large a share in the merit of
his discovery as most inventors or discoverers can
lay claim to. If the idea which has rendered him
famous was not in his mind at the outset of his
career of investigation, at any rate he had from
the first a desire for discovery, or, as he says
himself, the wish to know the secrets of this
world. It may be a question whether this impulse soon brought him to his utmost height of
survey, and that he then only applied to learning
to confirm his first views; or whether the impulse
merely carried him along with growing perception
of the great truth he was to prove, into deep
thinking upon cosmographical studies, Portuguese
discoveries, the dreams of learned men, the labours
of former geographers, the dim prophetic notices
of great unknown lands, and vague reports amongst
mariners of driftwood seen on the seas. But at
any rate we know that he arrived at a fixed conclusion that there was a way by the west to the
Indies; that he could discover this way, and so
come to Cipango, Cathay, the Grand Khan, and all
he had met with in the gorgeous descriptions of
Marco Polo and other ancient authorities. We

may not pretend to lay down the exact chrono-
logical order of the formation of the idea in his
mind, in fact, to know more about it than he
would probably have been able to tell us himself.
And it must not be forgotten that his enterprise,
as compared with that of the Portuguese along
the coast of Africa, was as an invention compared
to an improvement. Each new discovery then
was but a step beyond that which had preceded
it; Columbus was the first to steer boldly from
shore into the waste of waters, an originator, not
a mere improver.

Fernando Columbus divides into three classes
the grounds on which his father's theory was
based; namely, reasons from nature, the authority
of writers, and the testimony of sailors. He believed the world to be a sphere; he under-esti-
mated its size; he over-estimated the size of the
Asiatic continent. The farther that continent
extended to the eastward the nearer it came
round towards Spain. And this, in a greater
or less degree, had been the opinion of the ancient
geographers. Both Aristotle and Seneca thought
that a ship might sail "in a few days" from Cadiz
to India. Strabo, too, believed that it might be

possible to navigate on the same parallel of latitude, due west from the coast of Africa or Spain to that of India. The accounts given by Marco Polo and Sir John Maundeville of their explorations towards China confirmed the exaggerated idea of the extent of Eastern Asia.

But of all the works of learned men, that which, according to Ferdinand Columbus, had most weight with his father, was the "Cosmographia" of Cardinal Aliaco. And this book affords a good illustration of the then state of scientific knowledge. Learned arguments are interspersed with the most absurd fables of lion-bodied men and dog-faced women; grave, and sometimes tolerably sound, disquisitions on the earth's surface are mixed up with the wildest stories of monsters and salamanders, of giants and pigmies. It is here that we find the original of our modern acquaintance, the sea-serpent, described as being " of huge size, so that he kills and devours large stags, and is able to cross the ocean;" and the wonders of the unknown world are enunciated with a circumstantial minuteness which must have easily won the credence of a willing disciple like Columbus. He was also confirmed in his views of the exist

ence of a western passage to the Indies by Paulo
Toscanelli, the Florentine philosopher, to whom
much credit is due for the encouragement he
afforded to the enterprise. That the notices,
however, of western lands were not such as to
have much weight with other men is sufficiently
proved by the difficulty which Columbus had in
contending with adverse geographers and men of
science in general, of whom, he says, he never
was able to convince any one. After a new
world had been discovered, many scattered indi-
cations were then found to have foreshown it.
" When he promised a new hemisphere," writes
Voltaire, " people maintained that it could not
exist, and when he had discovered it, that it had
been known a long time." It was to confute
such detractors that he resorted to the well-
known expedient for making an egg stand on
end; an illustration of the meaning of originality
which, by the way, was not itself original, as
Brunelleschi had already employed it when his
merit in devising a plan for raising the cupola
of Florence cathedral was questioned.

Of the amount of evidence furnished by the
testimony of sailors, it is difficult to speak with

any degree of accuracy. Rumours of drift-wood, apparently carved with some savage implements; of mammoth reeds, corresponding with Ptolemy's account of those indigenous to India; even of two corpses, cast up on one of the Azores, and presenting an appearance quite unlike that of any race of Europe or Africa; all seem to have come to the willing ears of Columbus, and to have been regarded by him as " confirmations, strong as proofs of holy writ," of the great theory.

About the year 1470 Columbus arrived at Lisbon. According to the account given by his son, and adopted by the historian Bossi, he had sailed with Colombo el Mozo (the nephew of that " first Admiral of the family" of whom we have already heard) on a cruise to intercept some Venetian merchantmen on their way home from Flanders. At break of day the battle began, off Cape St. Vincent, and lasted till nightfall. The privateer commanded by Columbus grappled a huge Venetian galley, which, after a hand-to-hand struggle, caught fire, and the flames spread to the privateer. Friends and enemies alike sought safety in the sea, and Columbus, supporting himself on an oar, succeeded, when nearly exhausted,

in gaining the land, which was at some six miles'
distance.   God preserved him, says his son, for
greater things.

It was probably not long after this that he mar-
ried Donna Felipa Munnis Perestrelo, who was
residing at the convent of All Saints, in Lisbon,
where he was a regular attendant at the services
of the church.   She was a daughter of that captain of Prince Henry's who has been already mentioned as the first governor of Porto Santo. On
that island, after a short residence in the Portuguese capital, Columbus took up his abode, busying
himself with the papers of his deceased father-in-
law, and earning a livelihood by making maps
and charts for sale.   It is a curious fact that the
great chief of American discoverers should thus
have inhabited a spot which was the first advanced
outpost in African discovery.   He was here on
the high road to Guinea, and being in constant
communication with the explorers of the new
regions, it was likely that he would become im-
bued with some of their enthusiasm for adventure.

Shrouded in obscurity as this period of his life
remains, we are only able to find vague traditions

of the unsuccessful effort which Columbus made
to induce the Senate of Genoa to take up his
project. From the Portuguese crown he could
scarcely look for help, embroiled as it was in
costly wars, and having already a field for discovery along the African coast, which it would
scarcely be wise to forsake for an undertaking
similar in kind, but more hazardous and less defi-
nite. However, King John the Second, to whom
Columbus applied, seems to have listened with
attention to the exposition of his scheme, and indeed, according to the account of Fernando, to
have given a sort of qualified promise of his support, but to have disagreed with Columbus as to
terms. The king referred the matter to a Committee of Council for Geographical Affairs, before
whom Columbus laid his plans; but it is possible that even in the fifteenth century Boards
had come to regard projectors as their natural
enemies, and the report of the Committee was
entirely adverse to the scheme for Atlantic discovery. But it seems that the king was not
satisfied yet, whereupon the Bishop of Ceuta
(who had headed the opposition to Columbus in
the Council) suggested that a caravel should be

secretly equipped and sent out, with instructions founded on the plan laid before the committee. And this piece of episcopal bad faith was actually perpetrated. The caravel, however, returned without having accomplished anything, the sailors not having had heart to adventure far enough westward. It was not an enterprise to be carried out successfully by men who had only stolen the idea of it.

CHAPTER III.

Columbus in Spain.

COLUMBUS, disgusted at the treatment he had received from the Portuguese Court, quitted Lisbon for Spain, probably in the year 1485, with his son Diego, the only issue of his marriage with Donna Felipa, now no longer living. Here he addressed himself to the Duke of Medina Sidonia, and to the Duke of Medina Celi, whose extensive possessions along the coasts of Spain were likely to incline them in favour of a maritime expedition. There is some uncertainty as to the degree of encouragement which he received from them; but long afterwards, when Columbus had succeeded, the Duke of Medina Celi wrote to the Cardinal of Spain, showing that he (the duke) had maintained Columbus two years in his house, and was ready to

have undertaken the enterprise, but that he saw
it was one for the queen herself, and even then he
wished to have had a part in it. Probably, any man
in whose house Columbus resided for two years
would have caught some portion of his enthusiasm, and have been ready to take up his project.
It may be conjectured, however, that none of the
nobles of the Spanish court would have been
likely to undertake the matter without some sanc-
tion from the king or queen. To the queen,
accordingly, the Duke of Medina Celi addressed a
letter, of which Columbus was himself the bearer,
commending his enterprise to the royal favour.
But the juncture was singularly inopportune for
the consideration of any peaceful project. The
war with the Moors was raging more and more
furiously, as they were driven back, contesting
every inch of ground, farther and farther from the
heart of the kingdom. The court was now at
Cordova, actively preparing for the campaign
which was to result in that subjugation of the
crescent to the cross, throughout the Peninsula,
which was completed by the conquest of Granada
some six years later. Amid the clang of arms
and the bustle of warlike preparation, Columbus

was not likely to obtain more than a slight and superficial attention to a matter which must have seemed remote and uncertain. Indeed, when it is considered that the most pressing internal affairs of kingdoms are neglected by the wisest rulers in times of war, it is wonderful that he succeeded in obtaining any audience at all. However, he was fortunate enough to find at once a friend in the · Treasurer of the Household, Alonso de Quintanilla, a man who, like himself, " took delight in great things," and who obtained a hearing for him from the Spanish monarchs. Ferdinand and Isabella did not dismiss him abruptly. On the contrary, it is said, they listened kindly; and the conference ended by their referring the business to the Queen's Confessor, Fra Hernando de Talavera, who was afterwards Archbishop of Granada. This important functionary summoned a junta of cosmographers (not a promising assemblage!) to consult about the affair, and this junta was convened at Salamanca, in the summer of the year 1487. Here was a step gained; the cosmographers were to consider his scheme, and not merely to consider whether it was worth taking into consideration. But it was impossible for the jury to

F

be unprejudiced. All inventors, to a certain extent, insult their contemporaries by accusing them
of stupidity and of ignorance. And the cosmographical pedants, accustomed to beaten tracks,
resented the insult by which this adventurer was
attempting to overthrow the belief of centuries.
They thought that so many persons wise in nautical matters as had preceded the Genoese mariner
never could have overlooked such an idea as this
which had presented itself to his mind. Moreover, as the learning of the middle ages resided
for the most part in the cloister, the members of
the junta were principally clerical, and combined
to crush Columbus with theological objections.
Texts of Scripture were adduced to refute his
theory of the spherical shape of the earth, and the
weighty authority of the Fathers of the Church
was added to overthrow the "foolish idea of
the existence of antipodes; of people who walk,
opposite to us, with their heels upwards and
their heads hanging down; where everything is
topsy turvy, where the trees grow with their
branches downwards, and where it rains, hails,
and snows upwards." King David, St. Paul,
St. Augustine, Lactantius, and a host of other

theological authorities were all put in evidence against the Genoese mariner: he was confronted by the " conservatism of lawyers united to the bigotry of priests." Las Casas displays his usual acuteness when he says that the great difficulty of Columbus was, not that of teaching, but that of unteaching: not of promulgating his own theory, but of eradicating the erroneous convictions of the judges before whom he had to plead his cause. In fine, the junta decided that the project was " vain and impossible, and that it did not belong to the majesty of such great princes to determine any-thing upon such weak grounds of information."

Ferdinand and Isabella seem not to have taken the extremely unfavourable view of the matter entertained by the junta of cosmographers, or at least to have been willing to dismiss Columbus gently, for they merely said that, with the wars at present on their hands, and especially that of Granada, they could not undertake any new ex-penses, but when that war was ended, they would examine his plan more carefully.

Thus terminated a solicitation at the court of Ferdinand and Isabella which, according to some authorities, lasted five years; for the facts above mentioned, though short in narration, occupied no little time in transaction. During the whole of this period, Columbus appears to have followed the sovereigns in the movements which the war necessitated, and to have been treated by them with much consideration. Sums were from time to time granted from the royal treasury for his private expenses, and he was billeted as a public functionary in the various towns of Andalusia, where the court rested. But his must have been a very up-hill task. Las Casas, who, from an experience larger even than that which fell to the lot of Columbus, knew what it was to endure the cold and indolent neglect of superficial men in small authority, and all the vast delay, which cannot be comprehended except by those who have suffered under it, that belongs to the transaction of any affair in which many persons have to co-operate, compares the suit of Columbus to a battle, "a terrible, continuous, painful, prolix battle." The tide of this long war (for war it was, rather than a battle) having turned against him, Columbus left the court, and went to Seville "with much sadness and discomfiture." During this dreary period of a suitor's life—which, how-

ever, has been endured by some of the greatest
men the world has seen, which was well known
by close observation, or bitter experience, to
Spenser, Camöens, Cervantes, Shakespeare, Bacon — one joy at least was not untasted by
Columbus, namely, that of love. His beloved
Beatrice, whom he first met at Cordova, must
have believed in him, even if no one else had
done so; but love was not sufficient to retain
at her side a man goaded by a great idea, or
perhaps that love did but impel him to still greater
efforts for her sake, as is the way with lovers of
the nobler sort.

Other friends, too, shared his enthusiasm, and
urged him onward. Juan Perez de la Mar-
chena, guardian of the monastery of La Rabida,
in Andalusia, had been the confessor of Queen
Isabella, but had exchanged the bustle of the
court for the learned leisure of the cloister. The
little town of Palos, with its seafaring population
and maritime interests, was near the monastery,
and the principal men of the place were glad to
pass the long winter evenings in the society of
Juan Perez, discussing questions of cosmography
and astronomy. Among these visitors were Martin

Alonzo Pinzon, the chief shipowner of Palos, and Garcia Hernandez, the village doctor; and one can fancy how the schemes of Columbus must have appeared to the little conclave as a ray of sunlight in the dulness of their simple life. Hernandez, especially, who seems to have been somewhat skilled in physical science, and therefore capable of appreciating the arguments of Columbus, became a warm believer in his project. It is worthy of notice that a person who appears only once, as it were, in a sentence in history, should have exercised so much influence upon it as Garcia Hernandez, who was probably a man of far superior attainments to those around him, and was in the habit of deploring, as such men do, his hard lot in being placed where he could be so little understood. Now, however, he was to do more at one stroke than many a man who has been all his days before the world. Columbus had abandoned his suit at court in disgust, and had arrived at the monastery before quitting Spain to fetch his son Diego, whom he had left with Juan Perez to be educated. All his griefs and struggles he confided to Perez, who could not bear to hear of his intention to leave the

country for France or England, and to make a
foreign nation greater by allowing it to adopt
his project. The three friends—the monk, the
learned physician, and the skilled cosmographer—
discussed together the propositions so unhappily
familiar to the last named member of their little
council. The affection of Juan Perez and the
learning of Hernandez were not slow to follow
in the track which the enthusiasm of the great
adventurer made out before them; and they
became, no doubt, as convinced as Columbus
himself of the feasibility of his undertaking. The
difficulty, however, was not in becoming believers
themselves, but in persuading those to believe
who would have power to further the enterprise.
Their discussions upon this point ended in the
conclusion that Juan Perez, who was known to
the queen, having acted as her confessor, should
write to her highness. He did so; and the result
was favourable. The queen sent for him, heard
what he had to say, and in consequence remitted
money to Columbus to enable him to come to
court and renew his suit. He attended the
court again; his negotiations were resumed, but
were again broken off on the ground of the large-

ness of the conditions which he asked for. His opponents said that these conditions were too large if he succeeded, and if he should not succeed and the conditions should come to nothing, they thought that there was an air of trifling in granting such conditions at all. And, indeed, they were very large; namely, that he was to be made an admiral at once, to be appointed viceroy of the countries he should discover, and to have an eighth of the profits of the expedition. The only probable way of accounting for the extent of these demands and his perseverance in making them, even to the risk of total failure, is that the discovering of the Indies was but a step in his mind to greater undertakings, as they seemed to him, which he had in view, of going to Jerusalem with an army and making another crusade. For Columbus carried the chivalrous ideas of the twelfth century into the somewhat self-seeking fifteenth. The negotiation, however, failed a second time, and Columbus resolved again to go to France, when Alonzo de Quintanilla and Juan Perez contrived to obtain a hearing for the great adventurer from Cardinal Mendoza, who was pleased with him. Columbus then offered, in order to meet the objections of his opponents, to pay an eighth part of the expense of the expedition. Still nothing was done. And now, finally, Columbus determined to go to France, and indeed had actually set off one day in January of the year 1492, when Luis de Santangel, receiver of the ecclesiastical revenues of the crown of Aragon, a person much devoted to the plans of Columbus, addressed the queen with all the energy that a man throws into his words when he is aware that it is his last time for speaking in favour of a thing which he has much at heart. He told her that he wondered that, as she always had a lofty mind for great things, it should be wanting to her on this occasion. He endeavoured to pique her jealousy as a monarch, by suggesting that the enterprise might fall into the hands of other princes. Then he said something in behalf of Columbus himself, and the queen was not unlikely to know well the bearing of a great man. He intimated to her highness that what was an impossibility to the cosmographers, might not be so in nature. Nor, continued he, should any endeavour in so great a matter be attributed to lightness, even though the endeavour should fail ;

for it is the part of great and generous princes to
ascertain the secrets of the world. Other princes
(he did not mention those of neighbouring Portugal) had gained eternal fame this way. He
concluded by saying that all the aid Columbus
wanted to set the expedition afloat, was but a
million of maravedis (equivalent to about £308,
English money of the period); and that so great
an enterprise ought not to be abandoned for the
sake of such a trifling sum. These well addressed
arguments, falling in, as they did, with those of
Quintanilla, the treasurer, who had great influence
with the queen, prevailed. She thanked these
lords for their counsel, and said she would adopt
it, but they must wait until the finances had
recovered a little from the drain upon them occasioned by the conquest of Granada, or if they
thought that the plan must be forthwith carried
out, she would pledge her jewels to raise the
necessary funds. Santangel and Quintanilla
kissed her hands, highly delighted at succeeding;
and Santangel offered to advance the money required. Upon this the queen sent an alguazil to
overtake Columbus and bring him back to the
court. He was overtaken at the bridge of Pinos,

two leagues from Granada; returned to Santa Fé, where the sovereigns were encamped before Granada; was well received by Isabella; and finally the agreement between him and their catholic highnesses was settled with the secretary, Coloma.

Not much is seen of King Ferdinand in all these proceedings; and it is generally understood that he looked rather coldly upon the propositions of Columbus. We cannot say that he was at all unwise in so doing. His great compeer, Henry the Seventh, did not hasten to adopt the same project submitted to him by Bartholomew Columbus, sent into England* for that purpose by his

---

* It is difficult to determine how the project brought before Henry the Seventh's notice by Bartholomew Columbus was received. Some say it was made a mockery of at the English court; others speak of it as actually accepted. Lord Bacon states that Bartholomew was taken by pirates on his voyage to England, which delayed him so much that "before he had obtained a capitulation with the king for his brother, the enterprise by him was achieved." It is probable that Henry listened with interest to Bartholomew Columbus, who was a man of much intelligence and great maritime knowledge. But it seems unlikely that the negotiation went very far, considering the rigid manner in which Columbus insisted upon his exact conditions being accepted

brother Christopher; and it has not been thought to derogate from the English king's sagacity. Those who govern are in all ages surrounded by projectors, and have to clear the way about them as well as they can, and to take care that they get time and room for managing their own immediate affairs. It is not to be wondered at, therefore, if good plans should sometimes share the fate which ought to attend, and must attend, the great mass of all projects submitted to men in power. Here, however the ultimate event would justify the monarch's caution; for it would be hard to prove that Spain has derived aught but a golden weakness from her splendid discoveries and possessions in the new world.

---

by the Spanish court. No such bargain, at a distance, with a reserved and parsimonious monarch, was likely, therefore, to have been concluded. It appears, however, from a despatch from the Spanish ambassador to his sovereigns, dated the 25th July, 1498, that the English were not behind other nations in a thirst for discovery. "Merchants of Bristol," he says, " have for the last seven years sent out annually some ships in search of the island of Brazil and the Seven Cities." If this assertion is accurate, England must have anticipated Spain in the search for, though not in the discovery of, the western world.

Moreover, the characters of the two men being essentially opposed, it is probable that Ferdinand felt something like contempt for the uncontrolled enthusiasm of Columbus; and, upon the whole, it is rather to be wondered that the king consented to give the powers he did, than that he did not do more. Had it been a matter which concerned his own kingdom of Aragon, he might not have gone so far; but the expenses were to be eventually charged on Castille, and perhaps he looked upon the whole affair as another instance of Isabella's good natured sympathy with enthusiasts. His own cool and wary nature must have distrusted this " pauper pilot, promising rich realms."*

The agreement between Columbus and their Catholic highnesses is to the following effect:—

The favours which Christopher Columbus has asked from the King and Queen of Spain in recompense of the discoveries which he has made in the ocean seas, and as recompense for the voyage which he is about to undertake, are the following:—

---

* "Nudo nocchier, promettitor di regni."—*Chiabrera.*

1. He wishes to be made admiral of the seas and countries which he is about to discover. He desires to hold this dignity during his life, and that it should descend to his heirs.

This request is granted by the king and queen.

2. Christopher Columbus wishes to be made viceroy of all the continents and islands.

Granted by the king and queen.

3. He wishes to have a share, amounting to a tenth part, of the profits of all merchandise, be it pearls, jewels, or any other things, that may be found, gained, bought, or exported from the countries which he is to discover.

Granted by the king and queen.

4. He wishes, in his quality of admiral, to be made sole judge of all mercantile matters that may be the occasion of dispute in the countries which he is to discover.

Granted by the king and queen, on the condition, however, that this jurisdiction should belong to the office of admiral, as held by Don Enriquez and other admirals.

5. Christopher Columbus wishes to have the right to contribute the eighth part of the expenses of all ships which traffic with the new countries,

and in return to earn the eighth part of the profits.

Granted by the king and queen.
Santa Fé, in the Vega of Granada,
        April 17, 1492.

This agreement is signed by the Secretary Coloma and written by Almazan.

Then there is a sort of passport or commendatory letter intended for presentation to the Grand Khan, Prester John, or any other oriental potentate at whose territories Columbus might arrive :—

Ferdinand and Isabella to King ——.

The sovereigns have heard that he and his subjects entertain great love for them and for Spain. They are moreover informed that he and his subjects very much* wish to hear news from Spain; and send, therefore, their admiral, Ch. Columbus, who will tell them that they are in good health and perfect prosperity.

Granada, April 30, 1492.

---

* This crediting the unknown ruler with an anxiety for the welfare of the Spanish sovereigns is really a delicious piece of diplomatic affectation.

Armed with these royal commissions, Columbus left the court for Palos; and we may be sure that the knot of friends at the monastery were sufficiently demonstrative in their delight at the scheme on which they had pinned their faith being fairly launched. There was no delay in furnishing the funds for the expedition. From an entry in an account-book belonging to the Bishopric of Palencia, it appears that one million one hundred and forty thousand maravedis were advanced by Santangel in May, 1492, " being the sum he lent for paying the caravels which their highnesses ordered to go as the armada to the Indies, and for paying Christopher Columbus, who goes in the said armada." The town of Palos was ordered to provide two vessels.* But there

---

* The requisition to the municipality of Palos runs thus : " In consequence of the offence which we received at your hands, you were condemned by our council to render us the service of two caravels, armed, at your own expense, for the space of twelve months, whenever and wherever it should be our pleasure to demand the same." (30th April, 1492.) A proclamation of immunity from civil and criminal process to persons taking service in the expedition was issued at the same time. The ship of Columbus was, therefore, a refuge for criminals and run-

was still a weighty difficulty to be surmounted. It was no easy matter to obtain crews for such an expedition. The sovereigns issued an order authorizing Columbus to press men into the service, but still the numbers were incomplete, for the mariners of Palos held aloof, unwilling to risk their lives in what seemed to them the crazy project of a monomaniac. But Juan Perez was active in persuading men to embark. The Pinzons, rich men and skilful mariners of Palos, joined in the undertaking personally, and aided it with their money, and, by these united exertions, three vessels were manned with ninety mariners, and provisioned for a year.

The vessels were all of small size, probably of not more than one hundred tons' burden each, and, therefore, not larger than the American yachts, whose ocean race from New York to Cowes was regarded as an example of immense hardihood, even in the year 1867. But Columbus considered them very suitable for the undertaking. The

---

away debtors, a cave of Adullam for the discontented and the desperate. To have to deal with such a community was not one of the least of Columbus's difficulties.

G

Santa Maria, which Columbus himself commanded, was the only one of the three that was decked throughout. The official persons and the crew on board her were sixteen in number. The two other vessels were of the class called caravels, and were decked fore and aft, but not amidships, the stem and the stern being built so as to rise high out of the water. One of them, the "Pinta," was manned by a crew of thirty, commanded by Martin Alonzo Pinzon. The other, the "Niña," had Vincent Yanez Pinzon for captain, and a crew of twenty-four men. The whole number of adventurers amounted to a hundred and twenty persons, men of various nationalities, including, by the way, among them, two natives of the British Isles.

CHAPTER III.

First Voyage.

T length all the preparations were complete, and on a Friday (not inauspicious
in this case), the 3rd of August, 1492,
after they had all confessed and received the
sacrament, they set sail from the Bar of Saltes,
making for the Canary Islands. One can fancy
how the men and the women of Palos watched
the specks of white sails vanishing in the west,
and how, as each frail bark in turn disappeared
in the great ocean, mothers and sisters turned
weepingly away as if from a last farewell at the
grave of their sailor kinsmen.

Columbus was now fairly afloat, and we may
say with Milton, that—

> The world was all before him, where to choose.
> And Providence his guide.

His choice was made, however; and his Guide did not fail him.

He was about to change the long-continued, weary, dismal life of a suitor, for the sharp intense anxiety of a struggle in which there was no alternative to success but deplorable, ridiculous, fatal failure. Speaking afterwards of the time he spent as a suitor at court, he says, "Eight years I was torn with disputes, and in a word, my proposition was a thing for mockery." It was now to' be seen what mockery was in it. The following account of the voyage is mainly taken from an abridgment of Columbus's own diary made by Las Casas, who in some places gives the admiral's own words.

The little squadron reached the Canary Islands in a few days, with no event worth recording, except that the caravel "Pinta," commanded by Martin Alonzo Pinzon, unshipped her rudder. This was supposed to be no accident, but to have been contrived by the owners of the vessel, who did not like the voyage. The admiral (from henceforth Columbus is called "the admiral") was obliged to stay some time at the Canary Islands, to refit the "Pinta," and to make some change in the cut of her sails. While this was being done,

news was brought that three Portuguese government vessels were cruising in the offing with the
intention of preventing the expedition. However, on the 6th of September, Columbus set
sail from Gomera, and struck boldly out to sea,
without meeting with any of his supposed enemies.

In the abridgment of the diary, under the date
of the 19th of August, the admiral remarks that
many Spaniards of these islands, "respectable
men," swear that each year they see land; and
he remembers how, in the year 1484, some one
came from the island of Madeira to the King of
Portugal to beg a caravel in order to go and discover that land which he declared he could see
each year, and in the same manner. Had not
the admiral been conscious of the substantial
originality of his proceedings, he would hardly
have been careful to collect these scattered notices
which might afterwards be used, as many like
them were used, to depreciate that originality.
There is no further entry in the diary until the
6th of September, when they set out from Gomera
(one of the Canary Islands), on their unknown
way. For many days, what we have of the diary
is little more than a log-book, giving the rate of

sailing, or rather two rates, one for Columbus's
own private heed, and the other for the sailors.
On the 13th of September it is noted that the
needle declined in the evening to the north-west,
and on the ensuing morning, to the north-east,
the first time that such a variation had been
observed, or, at least recorded by Europeans.
On the 14th, the sailors of the caravel " Niña "
saw two tropical birds, which they said were
never wont to be seen at more than fifteen or
twenty leagues from shore. On the 15th they
all saw a meteor fall from heaven, which made
them very sad. On the 16th, they first came
upon those immense plains of seaweed (the
fucus natans), which constitute the Mar de Sar-
gasso, and which occupy a space in the Atlantic
almost equal to seven times the extent of France.
The aspect of these plains greatly terrified the
sailors, who thought they might be coming upon
submerged lands and rocks; but finding that the
vessels cut their way well through this sea-weed,
the sailors thereupon took heart. On the 17th,
they see more of these plains of seaweed, and
thinking themselves to be near land, they are
almost in good spirits, when finding that the

needle declines to the west a whole point of the compass and more, their hopes suddenly sink again: they begin " to murmur between their teeth," and to wonder whether they are not in another world. Columbus, however, orders an observation to be taken at day-break, when the needle is found to point to the north again; moreover he is ready with a theory sufficiently ingenious for that time, to account for the phenomenon of variation which had so disturbed the sailors, namely, that it was caused by the north star moving round the pole. The sailors are, therefore, quieted upon this head. In the morning of the same day they catch a crab, from which Columbus infers that they cannot be more than eighty leagues distant from land. The 18th, they see many birds, and a cloud in the distance; and that night they expect to see land. On the 19th, in the morning, comes a pelican (a bird not usually seen twenty leagues from the coast); in the evening, another; also drizzling rain without wind, a certain sign, as the diary says, of proximity to land.

The admiral, however, will not beat about for land, as he concludes that the land which these various natural phenomena give token of, can

only be islands, as indeed it proved to be. He
will see them on his return; but now he must
press on to the Indies. This determination shows
his strength of mind, and indicates the almost scientific basis on which his great resolve reposed.

Accordingly, he was not to be diverted from
the main design by any partial success, though by
this time he knew well the fears of his men, some
of whom had already come to the conclusion,
" that it would be their best plan to throw him
quietly into the sea, and say he unfortunately fell
in, while he stood absorbed in looking at the
stars." Indeed, three days after he had resolved
to pass on to the Indies, we find him saying, for
Las Casas gives his words, " Very needful for me
was this contrary wind, for the people were very
much tormented with the idea that there were no
winds on these seas that could take them back to
Spain."

On they go, having signs occasionally in the
presence of birds and grass and fish that land
must be near; but land does not come. Once,
too, they are all convinced that they see land:
they sing the " Gloria in excelsis;" and even the
admiral goes out of his course towards this land,

which turns out to be no land. They are like men listening to a dreadful discourse or oration, that seems to have many endings which end not: so that the hearer listens at last in grim despair, thinking that all things have lost their meaning, and that ending is but another form of beginning.

These mariners were stout-hearted, too; but what a daring thing it was to plunge, down-hill as it were, into

> " A world of waves, a sea without a shore,
> Trackless, and vast, and wild,*

mocked day by day with signs of land that neared not. And these men had left at home all that is dearest to man, and did not bring out any great idea to uphold them, and had already done enough to make them important men in their towns, and to furnish ample talk for the evenings of their lives. Still we find Columbus, as late as the 3rd of October, saying, " that he did not choose to stop beating about last week during those days that they had such signs of land, although he had knowledge of there being certain islands in that neighbourhood, because he would not suffer any

---

* Rogers.

detention, since his object was to go to the Indies; and if he should stop on the way, it would show a want of mind."

Meanwhile, he had a hard task to keep his men in any order. Peter Martyr, who knew Columbus well, and had probably been favoured with a special account from him of these perilous days, describes his way of dealing with the refractory mariners, and how he contrived to win them onwards from day to day; now soothing them with soft words, now carrying their minds from thought of the present danger by spreading out large hopes before them, not forgetting to let them know what their princes would say to them if they attempted aught against him, or would not obey his orders. With this untutored crowd of wild, frightened men around him, with mocking hopes, not knowing what each day would bring to him, on went Columbus. At last came the 11th of October, and with it indubitable signs of land. The diary mentions their finding on that day a table-board and a carved stick, the carving apparently wrought by some iron instrument. Moreover, the men in one of the vessels saw a branch of a haw tree with fruit on it. Now, in-

deed, they must be close to land. The sun went
down upon the same weary round of waters
which for so long a time their eyes had ached to
see beyond, when, at ten o'clock, Columbus,
standing on the poop of his vessel, saw a light,
and called to him, privately, Pedro Gutierrez, a
groom of the king's chamber, who saw it also.
Then they called Rodrigo Sanchez, who had been
sent by their highnesses as overlooker. I imagine
him to have been a cold and cautious man, of the
kind that are sent by jealous states to accompany
and curb great generals, and who are not usually
much loved by them. Sanchez did not see the light
at first, because, as Columbus says, he did not stand
in the place where it could be seen; but at last even
he sees it, and it may now be considered to have
been seen officially. "It appeared like a candle
that went up and down, and Don Christopher did
not doubt that it was true light, and that it was
on land; and so it proved, as it came from people
passing with lights from one cottage to another."

Their highnesses had promised a pension of ten
thousand maravedis to the fortunate man who
should see land first. The "Pinta" was the fore-
most vessel; and it was from her deck, at two

o'clock in the morning, that land was first seen by Rodrigo de Triana. We cannot but be sorry for this poor common sailor, who got no reward, and of whom they tell a story, that in sadness and despite, he passed into Africa, after his return to Spain, and became a Mahometan. The pension was adjudged to the admiral: it was charged, somewhat ominously, on the shambles of Seville, and was paid him to the day of his death; for, says the historian Herrera, " he saw light in the midst of darkness, signifying the spiritual light which was introduced amongst these barbarous people, God permitting that, the war being finished with the Moors, seven hundred and twenty years after they had set foot in Spain, this work (the conversion of the Indians) should commence, so that the Princes of Castille and Leon might always be occupied in bringing infidels to the knowledge of the Holy Catholic faith."

These last words are notable. They are such as Columbus himself would probably have made use of in describing this, the crowning event of his life. In the preface to his diary, which is an address to Ferdinand and Isabella, he speaks at large of the motives of their highnesses. He begins by saying how, in this present year of 1492, their highnesses had concluded their war with the Moors, having taken the great city of Granada, at the siege of which he was present, and saw the royal banners placed upon the towers of the Alhambra. He then tells how he had given information to their highnesses of the lands of India, and of a prince, called the Grand Khan, who had sent ambassadors to Rome, praying for doctors to instruct him in the faith; and how the Holy Father had never provided him with these doctors; and that great towns were perishing, from the belief of their inhabitants in idolatry, and from receiving amongst them "sects of perdition." After the above statement, he adds, "Your highnesses, as Catholic Christians and princes, lovers and furtherers of the Christian faith, and enemies of the sect of Mahomet, and of all idolatries and heresies, thought to send me, Christopher Columbus, to the aforesaid provinces of India to see the aforesaid princes, the cities and lands, and the disposition of them and of everything about them, and the way that should be taken to convert them to our holy faith."

Columbus then speaks of the expulsion of the

Jews from Spain as occurring at the same time as that in which he received orders to pursue a westerly course to India, thus combining the two transactions together, no doubt as proofs of the devout intentions of their highnesses: and, indeed, throughout the document, he ascribes no motives to the monarchs but such as were religious.

The diary to which this address was prefixed is probably one of the books which their highnesses allude to in a letter to Columbus, as being in their possession, and which they assured him they had not shown to anybody. I see no reason to doubt the perfect good faith of Columbus in making such a statement as that just referred to; and it is well to remark upon it, because we shall never come to a right understanding of those times and of the question of slavery as connected with them, unless we fully appreciate the good as well as the bad motives which guided the most important persons of that era.

As for Queen Isabella, there can be no doubt about her motives. Even in the lamentably unjust things in which she was but too often concerned, she had what, to her mind, was compelling reason to act as she did. Perhaps there is hardly any great personage whose name and authority are found in connection with so much that is strikingly evil, all of it done, or rather assented to, upon the highest and purest motives. Whether we refer to the expulsion of the Jews, the treatment of the Moorish converts, or the establishment of the Inquisition, all her proceedings in these matters were entirely sincere and noble-minded. Methinks I can still see her beautiful majestic face (with broad brow, and clear, honest, loving eye), as it looks down upon the beholder from one of the chapels in the cathedral at Granada: a countenance too expressive and individual to be what painters give as that of an angel, and yet the next thing to it. Now, I could almost fancy, she looks down reproachfully, and yet with conscious sadness. What she would say in her defence, could we interrogate her, is, that she obeyed the voice of heaven, taking the wise and good men of her day as its interpreters. Oh! that she had but persisted in listening to it, as it spoke in her own kindly heart, when with womanly pity she was wont to intercede in favour of the poor cooped-up inmates of some closely

beleaguered town or fortress! But at least
the poor Indian can utter nothing but blessings
on her. He might have needed no other " pro-
tector" had she lived; nor would slavery have
found in his fate one of the darkest and most
fatal chapters in its history.

But now, from Granada, and our fancies there,
the narrative brings us back to the first land
touched by Columbus. The landing of Columbus
in the New World must ever be a conspicuous
fact in the annals of mankind, and it was celebrated
by a ceremonial worthy of the occasion. On the
ensuing morning, after the light had been observed from the ships, being a Friday, the 12th of
October, 1492, Columbus, clad in complete armour,
and carrying in his hand the royal banner of
Spain, descended upon the level shores of the
small island* which had first greeted him, and
which he found to be very fruitful—fresh and
verdant, and " like a garden full of trees." The
other captains accompanied him, each of them
bearing a banner with a green cross depicted upon
it, and with the initials of Ferdinand and Isabella

* San Salvador, one of the Bahamas.

surmounted by their respective crowns—a device that well expressed the loyalty and devotion of Columbus, and had been chosen by him. These chief officers were followed by a large retinue from their crews. In numerous lines along the shore stood the simple islanders, looking on with innocent amazement.

On touching land, Columbus and all the Spaniards who were present fell upon their knees, and with tears—tears of that deepest kind which men do not know the cause of—poured forth their "immense thanksgivings to Almighty God."

The man who, of all that embassage, if we may call it so, from the Old to the New World, was certainly the least surprised by all he saw, was, at the same time, the most affected. For thus it is, that the boldness of a great design is never fully appreciated by the designer himself until he has apparently accomplished his work, when he is apt, if it be indeed a great work, to look back with shuddering awe at his own audacity in having proposed it to mankind. The vast resolve which has sustained such a man throughout his long and difficult enterprise, having for the moment nothing to struggle against, dies away, leaving a strange

H

sinking at the heart: and thus the greatest successes are often accompanied by a peculiar and bewildering melancholy. New difficulties, however, bred from success (for nothing is complete in life), soon arise to summon forth again the discoverer's energies, and to nerve him for fresh disappointments and renewed endeavours. Columbus will not fail to have his full share of such difficulties.

The followers of the great man, whose occasional faintheartedness must often have driven all sleep from his weary eyelids throughout the watches of the night, now began to think with remorse how much suffering they had needlessly inflicted upon their greatly-enduring leader. They sought his pardon with tears, and, subdued for the moment by his greatness when illustrated by success, expressed in loving terms their admiration, their gratitude, and their assurances of fidelity. The placable Columbus received their gracious sayings with all the warmth and tenderness that belonged to his large-hearted and amiable character.

The great business of the day then commenced; and Columbus, with the due legal formalities, took possession, on behalf of the Spanish monarchs, of

the island Guanahani, which he forthwith named
San Salvador. The gravity of the proceeding
must have astonished the beholding islanders.
Their attention, however, was soon turned to the
Spaniards themselves; and they approached the
strangers, wondering at their whiteness and at
their beards. Columbus, as being the noblest-
looking personage there present, and also from
wearing a crimson scarf over his armour, at-
tracted especial attention, and justly seemed,
as he was, the principal figure in this great
spectacle.

Columbus is for the present moment radiant
with success. Our interest passes now from him
to the new people he was amongst. And what
were they like? Were they worthy of the efforts
which the Old World had made to find them?
Was there mind and soul enough in them for
them to become good Christians? What says
the greatest of the men who first saw them?
What impression did they make on him? Let
him answer for himself:—

" Because they had much friendship for us,
and because I knew they were people that would
deliver themselves better to the Christian faith,
and be converted more through love than by

force, I gave to some of them some coloured caps and some strings of glass beads for their necks, and many other things of little value, with which they were delighted, and were so entirely ours that it was a marvel to see. The same afterwards came swimming to the ship's boats where we were, and brought us parrots, cotton threads in balls, darts and many other things, and bartered them with us for things which we gave them, such as bells and small glass beads. In fine, they took and gave all of whatever they had with good will. But it appeared to me they were a people very poor in everything. They went totally naked, as naked as their mothers brought them into the world."

Then Columbus goes on to say that these Indians were well made, with very good countenances, but hair like horsehair, their colour yellow; and that they painted themselves. They neither carried arms, nor understood such things, for when he showed them swords, they took hold of them by the blade, and hurt themselves. Their darts were without iron; but some had a fish's tooth at the end. In concluding his description, he says, " they ought to make faithful servants, and of good understanding, for I see that very quickly they repeat all that is said to them, and I believe they would easily be converted to Christianity, for it appeared to me that they had no creed."

A little further on, the admiral says of the people of a neighbouring island, that they were more domestic and tractable than those of San Salvador, and more intelligent, too, as he saw in their way of reckoning for the payment of the cotton they brought to the ships. At the mouth of the Rio de Mares, some of the admiral's men, whom he had sent to reconnoitre, brought him word that the houses of the natives were the best they had seen. They were made, he says, like "Alfaneques (pavilions), very large, and appeared as royal tents without an arrangement of streets, except one here and there, and within they were very clean, and well swept, and their furniture very well arranged. All these houses were made of palm branches, and were very beautiful. Our men found in these houses many statues of women, and several heads fashioned like masks, and very well wrought. I do not know, he adds, whether they have these for the love of the beautiful, or for purposes of worship." The Spaniards found also excellent nets, fish-hooks, and fishing-tackle. There were tame birds about the houses, and dogs which did not bark. " Mermaids," too, the admiral saw on the coasts, but thought them " not so like ladies as they are painted."

Speaking of the Indians of the coast near the Rio del Sol, he says that they are " very gentle, without knowing what evil is, neither killing nor stealing." He describes the frank generosity of the people of Marien, and the honour they thought it to be asked to give anything, in terms which may remind his readers of the doctrines maintained by Christians in respect of giving.

It is interesting to observe the way in which, at this point of the narrative, a new product is introduced to the notice of the old world, a product that was hereafter to become, not only an unfailing source of pleasure to a large section of the male part of mankind, from the highest to the lowest, but was also to distinguish itself as one of those commodities for revenue, which are the delight of statesmen, the great financial resource of modern nations, and which afford a means of indirect taxation that has, perhaps, nourished many a war, and prevented many a revolution. Two discoverers, whom the admiral had sent out from the Puerto de Mares (one of them being a learned Jew, who could speak Hebrew, Chaldee, and some Arabic, and would have been able to discourse, as Columbus probably thought, with any of the subjects of the Grand Khan, if he had met them), found that the men of the country they came to investigate, indulged in a "fumigation" of a peculiar kind. The smoke in question was absorbed into the mouth through a charred stick, and was caused by burning certain herbs wrapped in a dry leaf, which outer covering was called "tabaco." Las Casas, who carefully describes this process of imbibing smoke, mentions that the Indians, when questioned about it, said that it took away fatigue, and that he has known Spaniards in the island of Hispaniola who adopted the same habit, and who, being reproved for it as a vice, replied that it was not in their power to leave it off. "I do not know," he adds, "what savour or profit they found in them" (tabacos). I cannot help thinking that there were several periods in his own life, when these strange fumigations would have afforded him singular soothing and comfort. However that may be, there can be no doubt of the importance, financially and commercially speaking, of this discovery of tobacco; a discovery which, in the end, proved more productive to the Spanish Crown, than that of the gold mines of the Indies.

The excellent relations that existed between the expedition of Columbus and the inhabitants of Cuba may be seen from the fact that these two Christians, who were the first witnesses of tobacco-smoking, and who travelled with only two Indian attendants, were everywhere well and reverently received.

Resuming the thread of the history, it remains to be seen what more Columbus did and suffered in this voyage. The first Indians he met with had some few gold ornaments about them—poor wretches, if they had possessed the slightest gift of prophecy, they would have thrown these baubles into the deepest sea;—and they were asked whence came this gold? From a race, they said, living southwards, where there was a great king, who had much gold. On another occasion, other Indians being asked the same

question, answered, "Cubanacan, Cubanacan."
They meant the middle of Cuba; but their words
at once suggested to Columbus the idea that he
was now upon the traces of his long-looked-for
friend, Kublaï Kaan, the Khan of Khans. Indeed, it is almost ludicrous to see, throughout,
how Columbus is possessed with the notions
borrowed from his reading of Marco Polo and
other travellers. He asks for "his Cipango," as
Herrera slily puts it; and the natives at once
point out to him the direction where that is.
They thought he meant Cibao, where afterwards
the best mines of gold were found. The admiral,
bent on discovery, and especially on finding
the *terra firma*, which adjoined "his" India, did
not stay long anywhere. Proceeding southwards
from San Salvador, he discovered an island, or
rather a group of islands, to which he gave the
name of Santa Maria de la Concepcion; he then
discovered Cuba, and coasted along the north-
eastern part of that island; and afterwards, in
due course, came to Hispaniola, called by the
natives Hayti, in which island he landed upon
the territory of King Guacanagari, where he was
received most cordially.

Various conjectures have been made as to the different results which would have followed, both for the New and for the Old World, if Columbus had steered a little to the northward, or the southward, of the course which he actually took. One thing, however, is obvious, that in arriving at Hispaniola he came to a central point, not only of the West Indies, but of the whole of the New World, and a point, therefore, most felicitously situated for the spreading of future discovery and conquest.

It may be mentioned here, that Martin Alonzo Pinzon had wilfully parted company from the admiral while on the coast of Cuba : covetousness being probably the cause of this most undutiful proceeding. But, indeed, there is another instance of the insubordination of the mariners, which makes the wonder only still greater how Columbus could have brought them across the Atlantic at all. One evening the admiral, after paying a visit to Guacanagari, seeing the sea quite calm, betook himself to rest. As he had not slept for two days and a night, it is probable his slumber was deep. Meanwhile, the steersman, contrary to the distinct orders of the admiral, gave the helm to a common sailor, a youth. All the sailors went to sleep. The sea was as calm "as water in a dish." Little by little the ship drifted on to a shoal. Directly they touch, the sailor-boy at the helm starts from his dream, and gives the alarm. The admiral jumps up first (for the responsibility of command seldom goes quite to sleep); then the officer whose watch it ought to have been hurries up, and the admiral orders him to lower the boat which they carried on the poop. and to throw out an anchor astern. Instead of obeying the admiral, this cowardly villain, with others like him, sprang into the boat and made off for the other vessel, which was about half a league off. The other vessel would not receive them, and they rowed back again. But it was too late. The admiral did what he could in the emergency : he cut down the mast, lightened the vessel as best he might, took out his people and went with them to the other caravel, sending his boat to Guaca-nagari to inform him of the misfortune. The good Guacanagari was moved to tears by this sad affair. He gave not only sympathy, however, but assistance. His people went out with their canoes, and in a few moments cleared the vessel of all the goods in it. Guacanagari was very careful that nothing should be lost. He himself stood guard over the things which had been taken out of the ship. Then he sent comforting messages to the admiral, saying that he would give him what he had to make up for the loss. He put all the effects under shelter, and placed guards round them. The wrecker's trade might flourish in Cornwall; but, like other crimes of civilization, it was unknown in St. Domingo. The admiral was evidently touched to the heart, as well he might be, by the kindness of these Indians. He thus expresses himself, " They are a loving, uncovetous people, so docile in all things, that I assure your highnesses I believe in all the world there is not a better people, or a better country; they love their neighbours as themselves, and they have the sweetest and gentlest way of talking in the world, and always with a smile."

The admiral resolved to found a colony in Guacanagari's land, "having found such good will and such signs of gold." In relating this, the Spanish historian, Herrera, makes some curious reflections. He looks upon the loss of the vessel as providential, in order that the true faith might be preached in that country. Then he says, how providence causes its work to be done, not on high motives only, but also on the ordinary ones which influence mankind. He concludes by observing that providence dealt with the Indians as a prudent father who has an ugly daughter, but makes up for her ugliness by the help of a large dowry. By the ugliness in this case he means the seas to be traversed, the hunger to be endured, and the labours to be undertaken, which he considers no other nation but the Spaniards would have encountered, even with the hope of greater booty.

With the timber of the unfortunate " Santa Maria" Columbus built a fort, and called it La Navidad, because he entered the port near there, on Christmas-day. He remained on very friendly terms with the good Cacique Guacanagari; and might have established himself most advantageously in that part of the country, if he could have been content to be a settler. But from the first moment of his discovery he doubtless had an anxious desire to get back to Spain, and to tell what he knew; and at times, perhaps, was fearful lest his grand secret, through some mischance to the expedition, should still perish with him. The great discoverer, therefore, now prepared to return homewards. He left his fort in trust to a small body of his followers,* whom he commended to the good offices of Guacanagari, not forgetting to impress upon them the excellent advice, to do no violence to man or woman, and, in short, to make their actions conformable to the idea (which the Indians first entertained of them) that they had come from heaven: then, having received the necessary provisions for his vessel from the friendly cacique, the admiral set sail for Spain on the 4th of January, 1493.

---

* They were forty in number, and it would be strange to find, but for the well-known fact that nothing brings men of different races together more than maritime and commercial enterprise, that in this small list there is an Irishman, " Guillermo Ires" (*Qy.* William Herries, or Rice) " natural de Galney, en Irlanda;" and an Englishman, " Tallarte de Lajes" (*Qy.* Arthur Lake) "ingles."—NAVAR-RETE, *Col. Dip.*, Num. 13.

CHAPTER V.

Homeward bound.

OR two days Columbus stood to the eastward, but was met by a head-wind which prevented him from making much progress. On doubling the promontory of Monte Christo, however, the look-out at the mast-head made an announcement which was worth more than a fair wind to the voyagers, since it assured them that the homeward voyage of the "Niña" was not to be made without a consort; that the chance of the tidings of success being safely conveyed to Europe was not to depend upon the fortunes of a single ship. For, sailing down swiftly before the breeze which had detained Columbus, the "Pinta" hove in sight, and the two vessels

steered together into the bay of Monte Christo,
which Columbus had recently quitted. Pinzon, as
soon as the weather permitted, went on board the
admiral's caravel to account for his desertion,
which he stated to have been the accidental result of a storm which had driven him out of his
course and out of sight of his leader. The admiral accepted this explanation, as a quarrel with
Pinzon, whose townsmen and relations formed a
large proportion of the crews, might cause a
mutiny which would be fatal to the undertaking;
but he did not fail to note in his diary his conviction of Pinzon's bad faith. The fact was, that
Pinzon had heard from the natives of a certain
island, whence all the gold was said to come, and he
had wished to anticipate Columbus in the discovery
of this El Dorado, and to secure the profits for
himself. He had not found this home of the
gold, but had met with some natives from whom
he had obtained, by barter, a large quantity of
the precious metal. Half of this he had appro-
priated: the other half he had distributed among
his crew as a bribe to them to say nothing about
the matter.

After a few days spent in refitting the vessels,

and preparing for the homeward voyage, the Niña and her consort again set sail, coasting St. Domingo in an easterly direction as far as the Gulf of Samana. It was in this neighbourhood that the first affray with the aborigines took place, in consequence of an attack made by them upon an exploring expedition which Columbus had sent out. But so anxious was he to preserve a good understanding with the natives, that he did not leave the scene of the encounter until he had come to an amicable agreement with them. Another instance of the wise and humane policy by which he was actuated, is to be found in the fact, that on discovering that Pinzon had carried on board six natives to be taken to Spain, and there sold as slaves, he insisted on their release, dismissing them, moreover, with presents of such glittering toys as their kinsmen would be likely to appreciate, and as might predispose them in favour of the Europeans.

On the 16th of January, Columbus left the Gulf of Samana on his homeward course, from which, however, he deviated at first in the hope of finding the island, peopled with Amazons, described by Marco Polo, of which he had under-

I

stood the natives of St. Domingo to give him intelligence. Such a discovery would be, he considered, a conclusive proof of the identity of his new country with Marco Polo's Indies, and when four natives offered to act as his guides, he thought it worth while to steer (in the direction of Martinique) in quest of the fabulous Amazonians. But the breeze blew towards Spain; home-sickness took possession of the crews; murmurs arose at the prolongation of the voyage among the currents and reefs of those strange seas; and, in deference to the universal wish of his companions, Columbus soon abandoned all idea of further discovery, and resumed his course for Europe.

At first the voyage was tranquil enough, though the adverse trade-winds, and the bad sailing of the Pinta,* retarded the progress of both vessels. But on the 12th of February a storm overtook

---

* This was occasioned by the defective condition of her mast, whereupon the admiral remarks in his diary, that "if Pinzon had exerted himself as much to provide himself with a new mast in the Indies, where there are so many fine trees, as he had in running away from him in the hope of loading his vessel with gold, they would not have laboured under that inconvenience."

them, and became more and more furious, until, on the 14th, it rose to a hurricane, before which Pinzon's vessel could only drift helplessly, while the Niña was able to set a close-reefed foresail, which kept her from being buried in the trough of the sea. In the evening both caravels were scudding under bare poles, and when darkness fell, and the signal light of the "Pinta" gleamed farther and farther off, through the blinding spray, until at last it could be seen no more, when his panic-stricken crew gave themselves up to despair, as the winds howled louder and louder, and the seas burst over his frail vessel—then, indeed, without a single skilled navigator to advise or to aid him, Columbus must have felt himself alone with the tempest and the night. But his brave heart bore him up, and his wonderful capacity for devising expedients on sudden emergencies did not forsake him. As the stores were consumed, the Niña felt the want of the ballast which Columbus had intended to take on board at the Amazonian Island. "Fill the empty casks with water," he said, "and let them serve as ballast," an expedient which has grown common enough now, but which then was probably original.

Nor, while he did all that human skill could suggest for the safety of his vessel, did Columbus neglect to invoke the aid of that Higher Power, at whose special instigation he believed himself to have undertaken the expedition. With his whole crew he drew lots to choose one of their number to perform a pilgrimage to the shrine of Our Lady of Guadaloupe. The admiral was chosen. Twice more were lots drawn with a similar object, and once again the lot fell to the admiral. Afterwards, he and all the crew made a vow to go in procession, clothed in penitential garments, to the first church, dedicated to the Virgin, which they should meet with on arriving at land; and this vow, as we shall see presently, was followed by quite unexpected consequences.

When the chances of weathering the storm had become small indeed, Columbus determined that, if possible, the tidings of his discovery should not perish with him. He wrote a short account of his voyage on parchment, and this he enclosed in wax, and placed in a cask,* which he com-

---

* About the year 1852 a paragraph went the round of the English press announcing the discovery of this cask on

mitted to the waves. Thinking, probably, that his crew would interpret this as an abandonment of all hope, he concealed from them the real nature of the contents of the cask, so that they believed that their commander was performing some religious rite which might assuage the fury of the elements.

On the 15th of February the storm abated to some extent, and at last they came in sight of some land on the E.N.E., which the pilots held to be the Rock of Lisbon, but which the admiral more accurately determined to be one of the Azores. Vainly endeavouring, however, to make head against the wind and the sea, they lost sight of this island, but came in sight of another, lying more to the south, round which they sailed on the night of the 17th, but lost an anchor in endeavouring to bring up near the land. On the following day they cast anchor, and succeeded in communicating with the inhabitants, from whom

---

the African coast, by the barque "Chieftain," of Boston (Mass). Lamartine has accepted this story as correct, but it has never been authenticated, and there is a strong presumption in favour of its having been invented by some ingeniously circumstantial newspaper correspondent.

they learned that they had reached the island
of St. Mary, belonging to the Portuguese. The
governor sent amicable messages to Columbus,
and announced his intention of visiting him. But
when, in fulfilment of their vow, half the crew
went, barefoot and in their shirts, on a pilgrimage
to the chapel of St. Mary, which was not far from
the harbour, the governor and his satellites lay in
ambush on the road, and captured the whole band
of pilgrims. The crowns of Portugal and Castile
were still at peace, but it appears that this "man,
dressed in a little brief authority," thought that
the capture would gratify his sovereign. The
remonstrances of the admiral were of no avail;
and as the weather would not allow of his remaining in his present anchorage, he was forced to
stand out to sea, and to run nearly to St. Michael's,
with a crew which comprised only three able seamen. On the 21st of February he returned to
St. Mary's, and eventually, as the governor was
unable to seize Columbus himself, he decided on
recognizing the royal commission which he produced, and restoring his crew. On the 24th the
" Niña" again steered for Spain, but another
tempest supervened, and continued with more
or less fury for more than a week.

In this last storm, which raged with destructive violence along the west coast of the whole Continent of Europe, and which drove the " Pinta " almost helplessly towards a lee-shore, the dangers of the voyage reached their climax. " I escaped," says the admiral, " by the greatest miracle in the world." Fortunately, however, his seamanship was equal to the emergency, and on the afternoon of the fourth of March he came to anchor in the Tagus. To the King of Portugal, who happened to be at no great distance, he sent a despatch announcing his arrival and the result of his voyage, and, in reply, received a pressing invitation to court. With this he thought proper to comply, " in order not to show mistrust, although he disliked it," and was received by the king with the highest honours. This must have been almost too much of a triumph for a generous mind, considering that the court before which he was displaying the signs of a new world had refused the opportunity of securing the discovery for itself. The king, however, now took occasion to put in a claim to the newly found countries, basing it on that papal bull which has been mentioned in a previous chapter but, although Columbus, in the interest of his sovereigns, took care to repudiate this claim as decidedly as possible, his royal host continued to entertain him with the utmost consideration. Possibly mistrusting the seamanship of his subordinates, Columbus refused the offer of safe conduct and means of transport to Spain by land; and on the 13th of March, in the teeth of a north-westerly wind and a heavy sea, left the Tagus for the bar of Saltes, and safely reached his starting-point at Palos on the 15th, again a Friday. The enthusiasm and excitement aroused by the success of the expedition were unbounded. At Palos, especially, where few families had not a personal interest in some of the band of explorers, the little community was filled with extraordinary delight. Not an individual member of the expedition but was elevated into a hero,—not a debtor or a criminal whom the charter of immunity had led, rather than bear the ills he had, to fly to others that he knew not of,—but had expiated his social misdeeds, and had become a person of consideration and an object of enthusiasm. The court was at Barcelona. Immediately on his arrival Columbus despatched a letter to the king and queen, stating in general terms the success of his project; and proceeded forthwith to present himself in person to their highnesses. Almost at the same time, the " Pinta," which had been separated from her consort in the first storm which they encountered, made the port of Bayonne, whence Pinzon had forwarded a letter to the sovereigns, announcing " his" discoveries, and proposing to come to court and give full intelligence as to them. Columbus, whom he probably supposed to have perished at sea, he seems to have ignored utterly, and when he received a reply from the king and queen, directing him not to go to court without the admiral, chagrin and grief overcame him to such an extent that he took to his bed; and if any man ever died from mental distress and a broken heart, that man was Martin Alonzo Pinzon.

Herrera tells us that the admiral now " entered into the greatest reputation," and the historian goes on to explain to his readers what the meaning of "reputation" is. "It does not consist," he tells us, " in success, but in doing something which cannot be easily comprehended, which compels men to think over and over again about it." And certainly, this definition makes the word particularly applicable to the achievement of Columbus.

The court prepared a solemn reception for the admiral at Barcelona, where the people poured out in such numbers to see him that the streets could not contain them. A triumphal procession like his the world had not yet seen : it was a thing to make the most incurious alert, and even the sad and solitary student content to come out and mingle with the mob. The captives that accompanied a Roman general's car might be strange barbarians of a tribe from which Rome had not before had slaves. But barbarians were not unknown creatures. Here, with Columbus, were beings of a new world. Here was the conqueror, not of man but of nature, not of flesh and blood but of the fearful unknown, of the elements, and, more than all, of the prejudices of centuries. We may imagine the rumours that must have gone before his coming. And now he was there. Ferdinand and Isabella had their thrones placed in the presence of the assembled court. Columbus approached the monarchs, and then, "his countenance beaming with modest satisfaction," knelt at the king's feet, and begged leave to kiss their highnesses' hands

They gave their hands; then they bade him rise and be seated before them.   He recounted briefly the events of his voyage—a story more interesting than the tale told in the court of Dido by Æneas, like whom he had almost perished close to home,— —and he concluded his unpretending narrative by showing what new things and creatures he had brought with him.

Ferdinand and Isabella fell on their knees, giving thanks to God with many tears; and then the choristers of the royal chapel closed the grand ceremonial by singing the " Te Deum."   Afterwards men walked home grave and yet happy, having seen the symbol of a great work, something to be thought over for many a generation.

Other marks of approbation for Columbus were not wanting.   The agreement between him and the sovereigns was confirmed.   An appropriate coat of arms, then a thing of much significance, was granted to him in augmentation of his own.   In the shield are conspicuously emblazoned the Royal Arms of Castile and Leon.   Nothing can better serve to show the immense favour which Columbus had obtained at court by his discovery than such a grant; and it is but a trifling addition

to make, in recounting his new honours, that
the title of Don was given to him and his
descendants, and also to his brothers.   He
rode by the king's side; was served at table
as a grandee; "All hail!" was said to him on
state occasions; and the men of his age, happy
in that, had found out another great man to
honour.

The more prosaic part of the business had then
to be attended to.   The Sovereigns applied to
the Pope Alexander the Sixth, to confer on the
crowns of Castile and Leon the lands discovered
and to be discovered in the Indies.   To this
application they soon received a favourable
answer.   The Pope granted to the Princes of
Castile and Leon, and to their successors, the
sovereign empire and principality of the Indies,
and of the navigation there, with high and royal
jurisdiction and imperial dignity and lordship
over all that hemisphere.   To preserve the peace
between Spain and Portugal, the Pontiff divided
the Spanish and Portuguese Indian sovereignties
by an imaginary line drawn from pole to pole, one
hundred leagues west of the Azores and the Cape
de Verde Islands.

Meanwhile the preparations were being made for a second voyage to be undertaken by the admiral. After the arrival of the apostolic bulls, and before the departure of Columbus from Barcelona, the nine Indians brought by him were baptized. Here, parenthetically, we may take note of something which, if the fact did correspond with what the Spaniards thought about it, would, indeed, be notable. One of the Indians, after being baptized, died, and was, we are told,* the first of that nation, according to pious belief, who entered heaven.

We cannot help thinking of the hospitable and faithful Guacanagari, and imagining that, if his race had been like him, some one might already have reached the regions of the blessed. I do not, however, refer to this passage of Harrisse for its boldness or its singularity, but because it brings before us again the profound import attached to baptism in these times, and may help to account for many seeming inconsistencies in the conduct of the Spaniards to the Indians.

In the conduct, however, of Ferdinand and

* Harrisse.

Isabella towards the Indians there was nothing equivocal, but all that they did showed the tenderness and religious care of these monarchs for their new subjects. A special department for the control of colonial affairs was placed under the charge of Juan de Fonseca, an eminent ecclesiastic who was high in the royal favour, and on whom was eventually conferred the title of Patriarch of the Indies. But, unfortunately for the poor savages whose fate he was now to influence so largely, Fonseca's character had in it but little of the mild and forbearing spirit of Christianity. A shrewd man of business, a hard task-master, an implacable enemy, he displayed, during his long administration of Indian affairs, all the qualities of an unscrupulous tyrant, and was instrumental in inflicting on the islanders keener miseries than ever have been brought by conqueror upon a subject race.

Jealous of the rivalry of Portugal, the sovereigns took every means of hastening the preparations for a second voyage to be undertaken by the admiral. Twelve caravels and five smaller vessels were made ready, and were laden with horses and other animals, and with plants, seeds, and agricultural implements for the cultivation of the new countries. Artificers of various trades were engaged, and a quantity of merchandize and gaudy trifles, fit for bartering with the natives, were placed on board. There was no need to press men into the service now; volunteers for the expedition were only too numerous. The fever for discovery was universal. Columbus was confident that he had been on the outskirts of Cathay, and that the scriptural land of Havilah, the home of gold, was not far off. Untold riches were to be acquired, and probably there was not one of the 1500 persons who took ship in the squadron that did not anticipate a prodigious fortune as the reward of the voyage. Nor was one of the great objects of these discoveries uncared for. Twelve missionaries, eager to enlighten the spiritual darkness of the western lands, were placed under the charge of Bernard Buil, a Benedictine monk, who was specially appointed by the Pope, in order to ensure an authorized teaching of the faith, to superintend the religious education of the Indians. The instructions to Columbus, dated the 29th of May, 1493, are the first strokes upon that obdurate

mass of colonial difficulty which at last, by incessant working of great princes, great church-
men, and great statesmen, was eventually to be
hammered into some righteous form of wisdom
and of mercy.   In the course of these instructions, the admiral is ordered to labour in all
possible ways to bring the dwellers in the Indies
to a knowledge of the Holy Catholic Faith.   And
that this may the more easily be done, all the armada is to be charged to deal " lovingly" with the
Indians; the admiral is to make them presents,
and to " honour them much ; " and if by chance
any person or persons should treat the Indians
ill, in any manner whatever, the admiral is to
chastise such ill-doers severely.

Even at this early period of his administration,
Fonseca appears to have made some attempts to
thwart the admiral's wishes, attempts which
Columbus, now at the zenith of royal favour,
had no difficulty in baffling.   As regards the
household, for instance, Fonseca demurred to the
number of footmen which the admiral proposed
for his domestic establishment.   The admiral
appealed to the sovereigns, who allowed his claim,
and reproved Fonseca for objecting.

CHAPTER VI.

Second Voyage of Discovery.

N the 25th of September, all the preparations being complete, the squadron left Cadiz for the Canary Islands, and, after taking in provisions there, sailed from Ferro on the 13th of October. The voyage was singularly prosperous. There was but one storm, and that of not more than a few hours' duration; and favouring breezes wafted them over calm seas with a rapidity that brought the ships within sight of land on the 3rd of November, having made the voyage " by the goodness of God, and the wise management of the admiral, in as straight a track as if they had sailed by a well-known and frequented route." It was Sunday, and accord-

K

ingly the name of Dominica was given to the first island to which the admiral came.

From Dominica, where no aborigines were found, the admiral stood northward, naming one small island Maria Galante, after his own flagship, and calling a second and much larger one Guadaloupe, after a certain monastery in Estramadura. This island was peopled by a race of cannibals; and, in the houses of the natives, human flesh was found roasting at the fire. An exploring party from one of the ships penetrated into the interior, but so thickly was it wooded that they lost their way in the jungle, and only regained the ships after four days' wanderings, and when their safety was despaired of by their companions, who feared that they had become food for the savages. Fortunately, however, the men of the island were absent on some warlike expedition, and the white men only met with women and children in the course of their dangerous explorations.

Anxious to revisit the colony at La Navidad, the admiral proceeded north-westward as speedily as possible, and after passing and naming Montserrat, Antigua, St. Martin, and Santa Cruz, ar-

rived at a beautiful and fertile island which he
called St. John, but which has since received the
name of Porto Rico. Here were found houses
and roads constructed after a civilized fashion;
but proofs that the inhabitants were cannibals
abounded everywhere. On the 22nd of November the admiral reached the eastern end of
Hispaniola, and sailed along the northern shore
towards La Navidad, where a profound disappointment awaited him. The little colony
which he had founded had been entirely destroyed. The fort was razed to the ground.
Not one of the settlers was alive to tell the
tale. The account which Guacanagari gave to
Columbus, and which there seems no reason to
doubt, is, that the Spaniards who had been left
at La Navidad took to evil courses, quarrelled
amongst themselves, straggled about the country,
and finally were set upon, when weak and few in
numbers, by a neighbouring Indian chief named
Caonabo, who burned the tower and killed or
dispersed the garrison, none of whom were ever
discovered. It was in Caonabo's country that
the gold mines were reported to exist, and it is
probable that both the cupidity and the profligacy

of the colonists were so gross as to draw down upon them the not unreasonable vengeance of the natives.   Guacanagari, the friendly cacique, who had received the admiral amicably on his first voyage, declared that he and his tribe had done their utmost in defence of the Europeans, in proof of which he exhibited recent wounds which had evidently been inflicted by savage weapons.   He was, naturally, scarcely so friendly as before, but communication with him was made easy by the aid of one of the Indians whom Columbus had taken to Spain, and who acted as interpreter. Guacanagari was willing that a second fort should be built on the site of the first, but the admiral thought it better to seek a new locality, both because the position of the old fort had been un- healthy, and because the disgusting licentiousness of the settlers had offended the Indians to such an extent that whereas they had at first regarded the white men as angels from heaven, now they considered them as debased profligates and dis- turbers of the peace, against whom they had to defend their honour and their lives.

Sailing along the coast of Hayti, Columbus selected a site for his projected settlement, about

forty miles to the east of the present Cape Hay
tien.　This he called Isabella, after his royal
mistress.　Here the ships of his squadron dis-
charged their stores, and the Spaniards laboured
actively in the construction of the first town built
by Europeans in the New World.　But the work
did not progress prosperously.　Diseases prevailed
among the colonists.　The fatigues and discomforts
of a long sea voyage were not the best preparations for hard physical labour.　The number of
men which the admiral had brought out with him
was disproportionate to his means of sustaining
them.　Provisions and medicines began to fail.
And, worst of all, none of the golden dreams were
realized, under the influence of which they had
left Spain.　Only small samples of the precious
metal could be procured from the natives, and
the vaguely indicated gold mines of Cibao had
not been reached.　Anxiety, responsibility, and
labour began to tell upon the iron constitution of
the admiral, and for some time be was stretched
upon a bed of sickness.

　　Some idea of the difficulties which had to be
encountered at this period may be conceived from
an account of the state of his colony which Co-

umbus sent home in January 1494. It is in the form of instructions to a certain Antonio de Torres, the Receiver of the Colony, who was to proceed to the court of Spain and inform the monarchs of such things as were written in these instructions, and doubtless to elucidate them by discourse, as in the present day we send a despatch to be read by an ambassador to the foreign minister of the power we are treating with. There remains a copy, made at the time, of this document, and of the notes in the margin containing the resolutions of the sovereigns. The original, thus noted, was taken back to Columbus. It is a most valuable document, very illustrative of the cautious and wise dealing of the catholic sovereigns.

The document begins with the usual strain of complimentary address to great personages. *" Their Highnesses hold it for good service "* is the marginal remark.

The next paragraph consists of a general statement of the discoveries that have been made. *" Their Highnesses give much thanks to God, and hold as very honoured service all that the admiral has done."*

Then follow the admiral's reasons why he has

not been able to send home more gold. His people have been ill: it was necessary to keep guard, &c. " *He has done well*" is in the margin.

He suggests the building of a fortress near the place where gold can be got. Their Highnesses approve; and the note in the margin is, " *This is well, and so it must be done.*"

Then comes a paragraph about provisions, and a marginal order from the sovereigns, " *that Juan de Fonseca is to provide for that matter.*"

Again, there comes another paragraph about provisions, complaining, amongst other things, that the casks, in which the wine for the armada had been put, were leaky. Their Highnesses make an order in the margin, " *that Juan de Fonseca is to find out the persons who played this cheat with the wine casks, and to make good from their pockets the loss, and to see that the canes*" (sugar canes for planting, possibly) " *are good, and that all that is here asked for, be provided immediately.*"

So far, nothing can run more pleasantly with the main document than the notes in the margin. Columbus now touches upon a matter which intimately concerns the subject of slavery. He desires

his agent to inform their Highnesses that he has
sent home some Indians from the Cannibal Islands
as slaves, to be taught Castilian, and to serve
afterwards as interpreters, so that the work of conversion may go on.   His arguments in support of
this proceeding are weighty.   He speaks of the
good that it will be to take these people away
from cannibalism and to have them baptized, for
so they will gain their souls, as he expresses it.
Then, too, with regard to the other Indians, he
remarks, " we shall have great credit from them,
seeing that we can capture and make slaves of
these cannibals, of whom they (the peaceable
Indians) entertain so great a fear."   Such arguments must be allowed to have much force in
them; and it may be questioned whether many
of those persons who, in these days, are the
strongest opponents of slavery, would then have
had that perception of the impending danger of
its introduction which the sovereigns appear to
have entertained, from their answer to this part
of the document.   " *This is very well, and so it
must be done; but let the admiral see whether it
could not be managed there*" (i. e. in the Cannibal
Islands) "*that they should be brought to our Holy*

Catholic Faith, and the same thing with the Indians of those islands where he is."

The admiral's despatch goes much further: in the next paragraph he boldly suggests that, for the advantage of the souls of these cannibal Indians, the more of them that could be taken the better; and that, considering what quantities of live-stock and other things are required for the maintenance of the colony, a certain number of caravels should be sent each year with these necessary things, and the cargoes be paid for in slaves taken from amongst the cannibals. He touches again on the good that will be done to the cannibals themselves; alludes to the customs duties that their Highnesses may levy upon them; and concludes by desiring Antonio de Torres to send, or bring, an answer, " because the preparations here (for capturing these cannibals) may be carried on with more confidence, if the scheme seem good to their Highnesses."

At the same time that we must do Columbus the justice to believe that his motives were right in his own eyes, it must be admitted that a more distinct suggestion for the establishment of a slave-trade was never proposed. To their honour, Ferdinand and Isabella thus replied: *"As regards this matter, it is suspended for the present, until there come some other way of doing it there, and let the admiral write what he thinks of this."*

This is rather a confused answer, as often happens, when a proposition from a valued friend or servant is disapproved of, but has to be rejected kindly. The Catholic sovereigns would have been very glad to have received some money from the Indies: money was always welcome to King Ferdinand; the purchase of wine, seeds, and cattle for the colonists had hitherto proved anything but a profitable outlay; the prospect of conversion was probably dear to the hearts of both these princes, certainly to one of them: but still this proposition for the establishment of slavery was wisely and magnanimously set aside.

While Antonio de Torres was absent from Hispaniola, laying these propositions before Los Reyes, Columbus was busy about the affairs of the colony, which were in a most distracted state. Scant fare and hard work were having their effect; sickness pervaded the whole armament;

and men of all ranks and stations, hidalgoes, people of the court and ecclesiastics, were obliged to labour manually under regulations strictly enforced. The rage and vexation of these men, many of whom had come out with the notion of finding gold ready for them on the sea shore, may be imagined; and complaints of the admiral's harsh way of dealing with those under him (probably no harsher than was absolutely necessary to save them), now took their rise, and pursued him ever after to his ruin. A mutiny, headed by Bernal Diaz, a man high in authority, was detected and quelled before the mutineers could effect their intention of seizing the ships. Diaz was sent for trial to Spain. The colonists, however, were somewhat cheered after a time by hearing of gold mines, and seeing specimens of ore brought from thence; and the admiral went himself and founded the Fort of St. Thomas, in the mining district of Cibao. But the Spaniards gained very little real advantage from these gold mines, which they began to work before they had consolidated around them the means of living; in fact, dealing with the mines of Hispaniola as if they had been discovered in an old country, where the means of transit and supplies of provisions can, with certainty, be procured.

There was also another evil, besides that of inconsiderate mining, and, perhaps, quite as mischievous a one, which stood in the way of the steady improvement of these early Spanish colonies. The Catholic sovereigns had unfortunately impressed upon Columbus their wish that he should devote himself to further discovery, a wish but too readily adopted and furthered by his enterprising spirit. The hankering of the Spanish monarchs for further discovery was fostered by their jealousy of the Portuguese. The Portuguese were making their way towards India, going eastward. They, the Spaniards, thought they were discovering India, going westward. The more rapidly, therefore, each nation could advance and plant its standard, the more of much-coveted India it would hereafter be able to claim. Acting upon such views, Columbus now proceeded onwards, bent upon further discovery, notwithstanding that his little colonies at Isabella and St. Thomas must have needed all his sagacity to protect them, and all his authority to restrain them. He nominated a council to manage the government during his absence, with his brother Don Diego as president of it; he appointed a certain Don Pedro Margarite as captain-general; and then put to sea on the 24th of April, 1494.

CHAPTER VII.

IN the course of the voyage that then ensued, the admiral made many important discoveries, amongst them Jamaica, and the cluster of little islands called the "Garden of the Queen." The navigation amongst these islands was so difficult, that the admiral is said to have been thirty-two days without sleeping. Certain it is, that after he had left the island called La Mona, and when he was approaching the island of San Juan, a drowsiness, which Las Casas calls "pestilential," but which might reasonably be attributed to the privations, cares, and anxieties which the admiral had now undergone for many months, seized upon him, and entirely deprived him for a time of the use of his senses.

The object in going to San Juan was to capture cannibals there, and Las Casas looks upon this lethargical attack as a judgment upon the admiral for so unjust a manner of endeavouring to introduce Christianity. The mariners turned the fleet homewards to Isabella, where they arrived the 29th of September, 1494, bearing with them their helpless commander.

On Columbus's arrival at Isabella, where he remained ill for five months, he found his brother, Bartholomew Columbus, whose presence gladdened him exceedingly. His brothers were very dear to the admiral, as may be gathered from a letter to his eldest son Diego, in which he bids him make much of his brother Ferdinand, the son of Beatrice, "for," says he, "ten brothers would not be too many for you. I have never found better friends, on my right hand and on my left, than my brothers." Afterwards came Antonio de Torres with provisions, and all things needful for the colony. But nothing, we are told, delighted the admiral so much as the despatches from court, for he was a faithful, loyal man, who loved to do his duty to those who employed him, and to have his faithfulness recognized. Peace or delight, however, was not at any time to be long enjoyed by Columbus. He found his colony in a sad state of disorganization: the Indians were in arms against the Spaniards; and Father Buil, Don Pedro Margarite, and other principal persons had gone home to Spain in the ship which had brought Bartholomew Columbus.

The admiral, before his departure, had given a most injudicious command to Margarite, namely, to put himself at the head of four hundred men and go through the country, with the twofold object of impressing upon the natives a respect for the power of the Spaniards, and of freeing the colony from supporting these four hundred men. The instructions to Margarite were, to observe the people and the natural productions of the country through which he should pass; to do rigorous justice, so that the Spaniards should be prevented from injuring the Indians, or the Indians the Spaniards; to treat the Indians kindly; to obtain provisions by purchase, if possible, if not, by any other means; and to capture Caonabó and his brothers, either by force or artifice.

The proceedings of the men under Margarite were similar to the ? of the Spaniards formerly

left at La Navidad. They went straggling over
the country : they consumed the provisions of the
poor Indians, astonishing them by their voracious
appetites : waste, rapine, injury and insult followed in their steps; and from henceforth there
was but little hope of the two races living peace-
ably together in those parts, at least upon equal
terms. The Indians were now swarming about
the Spaniards with hostile intent : as a modern
historian describes the situation, " they had passed
from terror to despair;" and but for the oppor-
tune arrival of the admiral, the Spanish settlements in Hispaniola might again have been entirely swept away.

Caonabó, the cacique who, in former days, had
put to death the garrison at La Navidad, was now
threatening that of St. Thomas, the fort which
the admiral had caused to be built in the mining
district of Cibao. Guatignaná, the cacique of
Macorix, who had killed eight Spanish soldiers
and set fire to a house where there were forty ill,
was now within two days' march of Isabella, besieging the fort of Magdalena. Columbus started
up forthwith, went off to Magdalena, engaged the
Indians, and routed them utterly. He took a

L

large part of them for slaves, and reduced to obedience the whole of the province of Macorix. Returning to Isabella, he sent back, on the 24th of February, 1495, the four ships which Antonio de Torres had brought out, chiefly laden with Indian slaves. It is rather remarkable that the very ships which brought that admirable reply from Ferdinand and Isabella to Columbus, begging him to seek some other way to Christianity than through slavery, even for wild man-devouring Caribs, should come back full of slaves taken from amongst the wild islanders of Hispaniola.

Caonabó, not daunted by the fate of Guatignaná, still continued to molest St. Thomas. The admiral accordingly sallied out with two hundred men against this cacique. On the broad plains of the Vega Real the Spaniards found an immense number of Indians collected together, amounting, it is said, to one hundred thousand men. The admiral divided his forces into two bands, giving the command of one to his brother Bartholomew, and leading the other himself; and when the brothers made an attack upon the Indians at the same time from different quarters, this numerous host was at once and utterly put to flight. In speaking of such a defeat, the modern reader must not be lavish of the words " cowardly," " pusillanimous," and the like, until, at least, he has well considered what it is to expose naked bodies to firearms, to the charge of steel-clad men on horseback, and to the clinging ferocity of bloodhounds. A " horrible carnage" ensued upon the flight of the Indians. Many of them, less fortunate, perhaps, than those who were slain, being taken alive, were condemned to slavery. Caonabó, however, who was besieging the fortress of St. Thomas at the time of the battle on the Vega Real, remained untaken. The admiral resolved to secure the person of this cacique by treachery; and sent Ojeda (who afterwards became a conspicuous actor in the sad drama of conquest and depopulation in the West Indies) to cajole Caonabó into coming to a friendly meeting. There are some curious instructions of Columbus's to Margarite in 1494, respecting a plot to take this formidable Caonabó. They are as thoroughly base and treacherous as can well be imagined. This time the admiral's plan was completely successful.

The story which was current in the colonies,

of the manner in which Ojeda captured the resolute Indian chief, is this. Ojeda carried with him
gyves and manacles, the latter of the kind called
by the Spaniards, somewhat satirically, *esposas*
(wives), and all made of brass or steel, finely
wrought, and highly polished. The metals of
Spain were prized by the Indians in the same
way that the gold of the Indies was by the Spaniards. Moreover, amongst the Indians, there was
a strange rumour of talking brass, that arose from
their listening to the church bell at Isabella, which,
summoning the Spaniards to mass, was thought
by the simple Indians to converse with them.
Indeed the natives of Hispaniola held the Spanish
metals in such estimation that they applied to them
an Indian word, *Turey*, which seems to have sig-
nified anything that descends from heaven. When,
therefore, Ojeda brought these ornaments to Caonabó, and told him they were Biscayan *Turey*,
and that they were a great present from the admiral, and that he would show him how to put
them on, and that when they were put on Caonabó should set himself on Ojeda's horse and be
shown to his admiring subjects, as, Ojeda said,
the kings of Spain were wont to show themselves

to theirs, the incautious Indian is said to have fallen entirely into the trap. Going with Ojeda, accompanied by only a small escort, to a river a short distance from his main encampment, Caonabó, after performing ablutions, suffered the crafty young Spaniard to put the heaven-descended fetters on him, and to set him upon the horse. Ojeda himself got up behind the Indian prince, and then whirling a few times round, like a pigeon before it takes its determined flight, making the followers of Caonabó imagine that this was but display, (they all the while keeping at a respectful distance from the horse, an animal they much dreaded,) he darted off for Isabella, and after great fatigues, now keeping to the main track, now traversing the woods in order to evade pursuit, brought Caonabó bound into the presence of Columbus. The unfortunate cacique was afterwards sent to Spain* to be judged there; and his forces were presently put to flight by a troop of Spaniards under the command of this same Ojeda. Some were killed; some taken prisoners; some fled to the forests and the mountains; some

---

* He died on the voyage, however.

yielded, "offering themselves to the service of the Christians, if they would allow them to live in their own ways."

Never, perhaps, were little skirmishes, for such they were on the part of the Spaniards, of greater permanent importance than those above narrated, which took place in the early part of the year 1495. They must be looked upon as the origin in the Indies of slavery, vassalage, and the system of repartimientos. We have seen that the admiral, after his first victory, sent off four ships with slaves to Spain. He now took occasion to impose a tribute upon the whole population of Hispaniola. It was thus arranged. Every Indian above fourteen years old, who was in the provinces of the mines, or near to these provinces, was to pay every three months a little bellful of gold; all other persons in the island were to pay at the same time an *arroba* of cotton for each person. Certain brass or copper tokens were made—different ones for each tribute time—and were given to the Indians when they paid tribute; and these tokens, being worn about their necks, were to show who had paid tribute. A remarkable proposal was made upon this occasion to the admiral by Guarionex, cacique of the Vega Real, namely, that he would institute a huge farm for the growth of corn and the manufacture of bread, stretching from Isabella to St. Domingo (i. e. from sea to sea) which would suffice to maintain all Castile with bread. The cacique would do this on condition that his vassals were not to pay tribute in gold, as they did not know how to collect that. But this proposal was not accepted, because Columbus wished to have tribute in such things as he could send over to Spain.

This tribute is considered to have been a most unreasonable one in point of amount, and Columbus was obliged to modify his demands upon these poor Indians, and in some instances to change the nature of them. It appears that, in 1496, service instead of tribute was demanded of certain Indian villages; and as the villagers were ordered to make (and work) the farms in the Spanish settlements, this may be considered as the beginning of the system of *repartimientos,* or *encomiendas,* as they were afterwards called.

We must not, however, suppose that Indian slavery would not have taken place by means of Columbus, even if these uprisings and defeats of the Indian. in the course of the year 1495 had never occurred. Very early indeed we see what the admiral's views were with regard to the Indians. In the diary which he kept of his first voyage, on the 14th of October, three days after discovering the New World, he describes a position which he thinks would be a very good one for a fort; and he goes on to say, " I do not think that it (the fort) will be necessary, for this people is very simple in the use of arms (as your highnesses will see from seven of them that I have taken in order to bring them to you, to learn our language and afterwards to take them back); so that when your highnesses command, you can have them all taken to Castille or kept in the island as captives."

Columbus was not an avaricious, nor a cruel man; and certainly he was a very pious one; but early in life he had made voyages along the coast of Africa, and he was accustomed to a slave trade. Moreover, he was anxious to reduce the expenses of these Indian possessions to the Catholic sovereigns, to prove himself in the right as to all he had said respecting the advantages that would flow to Spain from the Indies, and to confute his enemies at Court.

Those who have read the instructions to Columbus given by the Catholic monarchs will naturally be curious to know how the news of the arrival of these vessels laden with slaves, the fruit of the admiral's first victory over the Indians, was received by the Sovereigns, recollecting how tender they had been about slavery before. This, however, was a very different case from the former one. Here were people taken in what would be called rebellion—prisoners of war. Still we find that Ferdinand and Isabella were heedful in their proceedings in this matter. There is a letter of theirs to Bishop Fonseca, who managed Indian affairs, telling him to withhold receiving the money for the sale of these Indians that Torres had brought with him until their Highnesses should be able to inform themselves from men learned in the law, theologians and canonists, whether with a good conscience these Indians could be ordered to be sold or not. The historian Muñoz, who has been indefatigable in his researches amongst the documents relating to Spanish America, declares that he cannot find that the point was decided; and if he has failed, we are not likely to discover any direct evidence about the decision. We shall hereaftei, however, find something which may enable us to conjecture what the decision practically came to be.

Many of the so-called free Indians in Hispaniola had, perhaps, even a worse fate than that which fell to the lot of their brethren condemned to slavery. These free men, seeing the Spaniards quietly settling down in their island, building houses, and making forts, and no vessels in the harbour of Isabella to take them away, fell into the profoundest sadness, and bethought them of the desperate remedy of attempting to starve the Spaniards out, by not sowing or planting anything. But this is a shallow device, when undertaken on the part of the greater number, in any country, against the smaller. The scheme reacted upon themselves. They had intended to gain a secure though scanty sustenance in the forests and upon the mountains; but though the Spaniards suffered bitterly from famine, they were only driven by it to further pursuit and molestation of the Indians, who died in great numbers, of hunger, sickness, and misery.

About this period there arrived in the Indies from the Court of Spain a Commissioner of In-

quiry, his mission being doubtless occasioned by
the various complaints made against the admiral
by Father Buil, Margarite, and the Spaniards
who had returned from Hispaniola. The name
of this commissioner was Juan Aguado, and his
powers were vouched for by the following letter
from the sovereigns:—

" The King and the Queen.

" Cavaliers, Esquires and other persons, who
by our command are in the Indies: we send you
thither Juan Aguado, our Gentleman of the
Chamber, who will speak to you on our part:
we command that you give him faith and credence.

" I the King: I the Queen.

" By command of the King and Queen, our Lords.

" HERNAND ALVAREZ.

" Madrid, the ninth of April, one thousand
four hundred and ninety-five."

The royal commissioner arrived at Isabella in
October, 1495, and his proceedings in the colony,
together with the fear of what he might report
on his return, quickened the admiral's desire to
return to Court, that he might fight his own

battles there himself.   For the tide of his fortune
was turning, and this appeared by several notable
signs.   Strong as was the confidence which the
Sovereigns reposed in him, the representations of
Margarite and Buil—the rough soldier and the
wily Benedictine — had produced their effect.
They complained of the despotic rule of Columbus; of the disregard of distinctions of rank which
he had manifested by placing the hidalgoes on the
same footing as the common men, as regards work
and rations, during the construction of the settlement ; and of his mania for discovery, which
made him abandon the colony already formed,
in the unremunerative search for new countries.   The commissioner who was sent to investigate these charges, as well as to report on
the condition of the colony, found no difficulty in
collecting evidence to substantiate them.   An
unsuccessful man is generally persuaded that
somebody else has caused his failure.   And the
" somebody else," in the case of the colonists,
was, by universal consent, the foreign sea-captain
who had deluded Spanish hidalgoes by his wild
projects, and had become a grandee under false
pretences.   The Indians, too, who were glad to

lay their miseries at the door of somebody, and who were told that Aguado was the new admiral, and had come to supplant the old one, were not slow to add their quota to the charges against Columbus. To rebut these accusations, as well as to protest against the issue of licences, to private adventurers, to trade in the new countries independently of the admiral (a measure which, in violation of Columbus's charter, had lately been adopted by Fonseca) he quitted Isabella on the 10th of March, 1496, in the " Niña," while Aguado took ship in another caravel. Many of the colonists, who had been rudely awakened from their golden dreams, seized this opportunity of returning to Spain ; and the Cacique Caonabó was also on board, probably with a view of impressing upon him an overwhelming conviction of Spanish power, and of the futility of any efforts to resist it.

The voyage was a miserable one. Contrary winds prevailed until provisions began to run short, and rations were doled out in pittances which grew scantier and scantier until all the admiral's authority was needed to prevent his ravenous shipmates from killing and eating the

Caribs who were on board,—in retribution, so ran
the grim jest, for their cannibalism.   At last,
when famine was imminent, after a voyage of three
months' duration, the two caravels entered the
Bay of Cadiz on the 11th of June, 1496.   After
about a month's delay, Columbus received a sum-
mons to proceed to the Court, which was then at
Burgos.   In the course of his journey thither he
adopted the same means of dazzling the eyes of
the populace, by the display of gold and the ex-
hibition of his captives, as on his return from his
first voyage; but so many unsuccessful colonists
had returned, sick at heart and ruined in health,
to tell the tale of failure to their countrymen, that
this triumphal procession was very unlike the
last as regards the welcome accorded by the
public.   However the Sovereigns seem to have
given the admiral a kind reception, and instead
of placing him on his defence against the charges
which had been brought forward by Father Buil,
they listened with sympathy to his story of the difficulties which had beset him, and heard with
sanguine satisfaction of the recent discovery of the
mines from which it was said that the natives
procured most of the gold that had been found

in their possession, and which promised an incalculably rich harvest. Presently, in apparent confirmation of this belief, one Pedro Nino, a captain of the admiral's, announced his arrival at Cadiz, with a quantity of "gold in bars" on board his ship. It was not until great expectations had been raised at Court, and the wildest ideas conceived of the magnitude of this supposed first instalment of the riches of the newly found gold mines, that it turned out that this Nino was merely a miserable maker of jokes, and that the "gold *in bars*" was only represented by the Indians who composed his cargo, whose present captivity was secured by " bars," and whose future sale was to furnish gold. This absurdity naturally caused Columbus and his friends no slight mortification, and added a fresh weapon to the shafts of ridicule which his enemies were for ever launching at his extravagant theories and his expensive projects.

CHAPTER VIII.

DURING the two years that elapsed from the Admiral's leaving Hispaniola in 1496 to his return there in 1498, many things happened on both sides the Atlantic, which need recording. In 1496 we find, that Don Bartholomew Columbus sent to Spain three hundred slaves from Hispaniola. He had previously informed the Sovereigns that certain caciques were killing the Castilians, and their Highnesses had given orders in reply, that all those who should be found guilty should be sent to Spain. If this meant the common Indians as well as the caciques, then it seems probable that the question about selling them with a safe conscience was already decided.

In 1497, two very injudicious edicts were published by the Catholic Sovereigns, upon the advice, as we are told, of Columbus; one, authorizing the judges to transport criminals to the Indies; the other, giving an indulgence to all those who had committed any crime (with certain exceptions, among which heresy, *lèse majesté*, and treason, find a place) to go out at their own expense to Hispaniola, and to serve for a certain time under the orders of the admiral. The remembrance of this advice on his part, might well have shamed · Columbus from saying, as he did three years afterwards, in his most emphatic manner, " I swear that numbers of men have gone to the Indies who did not deserve water from God or man." It is but fair, however, to mention, that Las Casas, speaking of the colonists who went out under these conditions, says, " I have known some of them in these islands, even of those who had lost their ears, whom I always found sufficiently honest men."

In 1497, letters patent were issued from the Sovereigns to the admiral, authorizing him to grant *repartimientos* of the lands in the Indies to the Spaniards. It is noticeable that in this document there is no mention of Indians, so that they had

M

not come to form portion of a *repartimiento* at this period. The document in question is of a formal character, expressed in the style of legal documents of the present day, by virtue of which the fortunate Spaniard who gets the land is " to have, and to hold, and to possess," and so forth ; and is enabled " to sell and to give, and to present, and to traffic with, and to exchange, and to pledge, and to alienate, and to do with it and in it all that he likes or may think good."

While the acts of legislation above narrated, which cannot be said to have been favourable to good government in the Indies, were being framed at the Court of Spain, Don Bartholomew Columbus was doing much in his administration of Hispaniola that led to very mischievous results.

Before the admiral left the island, he had discovered some mines to the southward, and had thought of choosing a port in their vicinity, where he might establish a colony. He had spoken about this in his letters to the Government at home. As he entered the Bay of Cadiz on his return, he met some vessels there, which were bound for Hispaniola, and which contained letters from their Highnesses approving of his suggestion.

By these ships, therefore, he sent orders to his brother to make this southern settlement; and the " Adelantado " accordingly proceeded southwards, and fixed upon a port at the entrance of the river Ozama. He sent for artizans from Isabella, and commenced building a fortress, which he called St. Domingo, and which afterwards became the chief port of the island.

There was one part of Hispaniola into which the Spaniards had not yet penetrated: it was called Xaragua, and was reigned over by a Cacique named Bohechio, whose sister, Anacaona, the wife of Caonabo, and a noted beauty, seems also to have had much authority in those parts. The Adelantado, after seeing the works at St. Domingo commenced, resolved to enter the kingdom of Xaragua, whither he proceeded at the head of one hundred men. Arriving at the river Neyba, he found an immense army of Indians drawn up there to oppose his progress. Don Bartholomew made signs to them that his errand was peaceful; and the good-natured Indians accepting his proffers of amity, he was conducted some thirty leagues further to the city of Xaragua, where he was received with processions of dancing and singing women, and feasted magnificently. After having been well entertained by these Indians, the " Adelantado " proceeded to business, and, in plain terms, demanded tribute of them. Bohechio pleaded that there was no gold in his dominions, to which the Adelantado replied that he did not wish to impose tribute upon any people, except of the natural productions to be found in their country. It was finally settled that Bohechio should pay tribute in cotton and cazabi-bread. He acceded to this agreement very willingly; and the Adelantado and this cacique parted on the most friendly terms.

Don Bartholomew then returned to Isabella, where he found that about three hundred men had died from disease, and that there was great dearth of provisions. He distributed the sick men in his fortresses, and in the adjacent Indian villages, and afterwards set out on a journey to his new fort of St. Domingo, collecting tribute by the way. In all these rapid and energetic proceedings of the Adelantado, and still more from causes over which he had no control, the Spaniards must have suffered much; and, doubtless, those complaints on their part, which were soon to break out very menacingly, were not unheard at the present time.

If the Spaniards, however, complained of the labours which Don Bartholomew imposed upon them, the Indians complained still more, and far more justly, of the tribute imposed upon them. Several of the minor chiefs, upon this occasion of collecting tribute, complained to the great Cacique Guarionex, and suggested a rising of the Indians. This cacique seems to have been a peaceful, prudent man, and well aware of the power of the Spaniards. But he now consented to place himself at the head of an insurrection, which, however, the lieutenant-governor, soon made aware of it, quelled at once by a battle in which he was victorious over Guarionex, taking him and other principal persons captive. The chief movers of the revolt were put to death; but Guarionex was delivered up to his people, who flocked by thousands to his place of imprisonment, clamouring for his restitution.

About this time messengers came from Bohechio and Anacaona, informing the Adelantado that the tribute of that country was ready for him, and he accordingly went to fetch it. During his absence from the seat of government, and under the less vigorous administration of Don Diego Columbus, who had been left at the head of affairs at Isabella, those discontents among the Spaniards, which had no doubt been rife for a long time, broke out in a distinct manner. I allude to the well-known insurrection of Roldan, whom the admiral, on his departure, had left as chief justice in the island. The disputes between the chief justice and the governor were to form the first of a series of similar proceedings to take place afterwards in many colonies even down to our own times. It may be imagined that the family of Columbus were a hard race to deal with; and any one observing that the admiral was very often engaged in disputes, and almost always in the right, might conjecture that he was one of those persons who pass through life proving that all people about them are wrong, and going a great way to make them so. This would have been an easy mode of explaining many things, and therefore very welcome to a narrator, but it would not be at all just towards Columbus to saddle upon him any such character. Here were men who had come out with very grand expectations, and who found themselves pinched with hunger, having dire storms to encounter, and vast labours to undergo; who were restrained within due bounds by no pressure of society; who were commanded by a foreigner, or by members of his family, whom they knew to have many enemies at court; who thought that the Sovereigns themselves could scarcely reach them at this distance; and who imagined that they had worked themselves out of all law and order, and that they deserved an Alsatian immunity. With such men (many of them, perhaps, "not worthy of water,") the admiral and his brothers had to get useful works of all kinds done; and did contrive to get vessels navigated, forts built, and some ideas of civilization maintained. But it was an arduous task at all times: and this Roldan did not furnish the least of the troubles which the admiral and his brothers had to endure.

Roldan, too, if we could hear him, would probably have something to say. He wished, it appears, to return to Spain, as Father Buil and Margarite had done; and urged that a certain caravel which the Governor Don Bartholomew Columbus had built, might be launched for that

purpose.   Such is the account of Ferdinand Columbus, who maintains that the said caravel could
not be launched for want of tackle.   He also
mentions that Roldan complained of the restless
life the Adelantado led his men, building forts
and towns ; and said that there was no hope of
the admiral coming back to the colony with supplies.   Without going into these squabbles—and
indeed it is very difficult when a quarrel of this
kind arises, taking it up at the point where it
breaks out, to judge it upon that only, since the
stream of ill-will may have run underground for
a long time—suffice it to say, that Roldan and his
men grew more and more insubordinate ; were not
at all quelled by the presence of the Adelantado
on his return from Xaragua ; and finally quitted
Isabella in a body.   The Adelantado contrived to
keep some men faithful to him, promising them,
amongst other things, two slaves each.   Negotiations then took place between the Adelantado
and Roldan, which must be omitted for the present, to enter upon the further dealing of Don
Bartholomew with the Indians.

  These poor islanders were now harassed both
by the rebels and by the loyal Spaniards, whom

the Adelantado could not venture to curb much, for fear of their going over to the other party. The Indians were also tempted by Roldan to join him, as he contended that tribute had been unjustly imposed upon them. From all these difficulties, Guarionex made his escape by flying to the territories of Maiobanex, the cacique of a hardy race, who inhabited the hilly country towards Cabron. This flight of Guarionex was a very serious affair, as it threatened the extinction of tribute in that cacique's territory ; and Don Bartholomew accordingly pursued the fugitive. After some skirmishes with the troops of Maiobanex, in which, as usual, the Spaniards were victorious, the Adelantado sent a messenger to Maiobanex, telling him that the Spaniards did not seek war with him, but that he must give up Guarionex, otherwise his own territory would be destroyed by fire and sword. Maiobanex replied, that every one knew that Guarionex was a good man, endowed with all virtue, wherefore he judged him to be worthy of assistance and defence, but that they, the Spaniards, were violent and bad men, and that he would have neither friendship nor commerce with them.

Upon receiving this answer, the Adelantado burnt several villages, and approached nearer to the camp of Maiobanex. Fresh negotiations were entered into: Maiobanex convoked an assembly of his people; and they contended that Guarionex ought to be given up, and cursed the day when first he came amongst them. Their noble chief, however, said, " that Guarionex was a good man, and deserved well at his hands, for he had given him many royal gifts when he came to him, and had taught him and his wife to join in choral songs and to dance, of which he made no little account; and for which he was grateful: wherefore, he would be party to no treaty to desert Guarionex, since he had fled to him, and he had pledged himself to take care of the fugitive; and would rather suffer all extremities than give detractors a cause for speaking ill, to say that he had delivered up his guest." The assemblage of the people being dismissed, Maiobanex informed his guest that he would stand by him to the last.

The fugitive cacique, however, finding that Maiobanex's people were ill-disposed towards him, quitted, of his own accord, their territory; but by so doing, he was not enabled to save his generous

host, who, with his family, was surprized and
taken ; and Guarionex himself being shortly afterwards captured and put in chains at Fort Concep-
çion, the two caciques probably shared the same
prison.   Thus concludes a story, which, if it had
been written by some Indian Plutarch, and the
names had been more easy to pronounce, might
have taken its just place amongst the familiar and
household stories which we tell our children, to
make them see the beauty of great actions.

CHAPTER IX.

A GOOD starting-point for that important part of the narrative which comes next —namely, the discovery of the American continent by Columbus—will be a recital of the first clause in the instructions given by Ferdinand and Isabella to the admiral, in the year 1497, previously to his undertaking his third voyage—a voyage which, though not to be compared to his first one, is still very memorable, on account of the discoveries he made, and the sufferings he experienced in the course of it.

The first clause of the instructions is to the effect, that the Indians of the islands are to be brought into peace and quietude, being reduced into subjection "benignantly;" and also, as the principal end of the conquest, that they be converted to the sacred Catholic Faith, and have the holy Sacraments administered to them.

It will be needless to recount the vexations of that "much-enduring man," Columbus, before his embarkation. Suffice it to say, that he set sail from the port of San Lucar on the 30th of May, 1498, with six vessels, and two hundred men, in addition to the sailors that were necessary to navigate the vessels. In the course of his voyage he was obliged to avoid a French squadron which was cruizing in those seas, as France and Spain were then at war. From Gomera, one of the Canary islands, he despatched three of his ships directly to Hispaniola, declaring in his instructions to their commanders, that he was going to the Cape Verde islands, and thence, "in the name of the Sacred Trinity," intended to navigate to the south of those islands, until he should arrive under the equinoctial line, in the hope of being "guided by God to discover something which may be to His service, and to that of our Lords, the King and Queen, and to the honour of Christendom;" "for, I believe," he adds, "that no one has ever traversed this way, and that this sea is nearly unknown."

With one ship, therefore, and two caravels, the great admiral made for the Cape Verde islands, "a false name," as he observes, for nothing was to be seen there of a green colour. He reached these islands on the 27th of June, and quitted them on the 4th of July, having been in the midst of such a dense fog all the time, that, he says, "it might have been cut with a knife." Thence he proceeded to the south-west, intending afterwards to take a westerly direction. When he had gone, as he says, one hundred and twenty leagues, he began to find those floating fields of sea-weed which he had encountered in his first voyage. Here he took an observation at nightfall, and found that the north star was in five degrees. The wind suddenly abated, and the heat was intolerable; so much so, that nobody dared to go below deck to look after the wine and the provisions. This extraordinary heat lasted eight days. The first day was clear, and if the others had been like it, the admiral says, not a man would have been left alive, but they would all have been burnt up.

At last a favourable breeze sprang up, enabling the admiral to take a westerly course, the one he

most desired, as he had before noticed in his voyages to the Indies that about a hundred miles west
of the Azores there was always a sudden change of
temperature.* On Sunday, the 22nd of July, in
the evening, the sailors saw innumerable birds
going from the south-west to the north-east,
which flight of birds was a sign that land was not
far off. For several successive days birds were
seen, and an albatross perched upon the admiral's
vessel. Still the fleet went on without seeing
land, and, as it was in want of fresh water, the
admiral was thinking of changing his course, and,
indeed, on Thursday, the 31st of July, had commenced steering northwards for some hours, when,
to use his own words, " as God had always been
accustomed to show mercy to him," a certain
mariner of Huelva, a follower of the admiral's,
named Alonzo Perez, happened to go up aloft
upon the maintop-sail of the admiral's ship, and
suddenly saw land towards the south-west, about

---

* I suppose he came into or out of one of those warm
ocean rivers which have so great an effect in modifying the
temperature of the earth—perhaps into the one which comes
from the south of Africa through the Gulf of Mexico, to
our own shores, and on which we so much depend.

fifteen leagues off. This land which he described was in the form of three lofty hills or mountains. It would be but natural to conjecture that, as Columbus had resolved to name the first land he should discover " Trinidad," it was by an effort of the will, or of the imagination, that these three eminences were seen first; but it is exceedingly probable that such eminences were to be seen from the point whence Alonzo Perez first saw land.*

The sailors sung the " Salve Regina," with other pious hymns in honour of God and " Our Lady," according to the custom of the mariners of Spain, who, in terror or in joy, were wont to find an expression for their feelings in such sacred canticles.

The admiral's course, when he was going northwards, had been in the direction of the Carib islands, already well known to him; but with great delight he now turned towards Trinidad, making for a cape, which, from the likeness of a little rocky islet near it to a galley in full sail, he

---

* Cape Cashepou is backed by three peaked mountains, of which a representation is given in DAY's *West Indies*, vol. 2, p. 31.

named " La Galera."* There he arrived "at the
hour of complines," but, not finding the port suf-

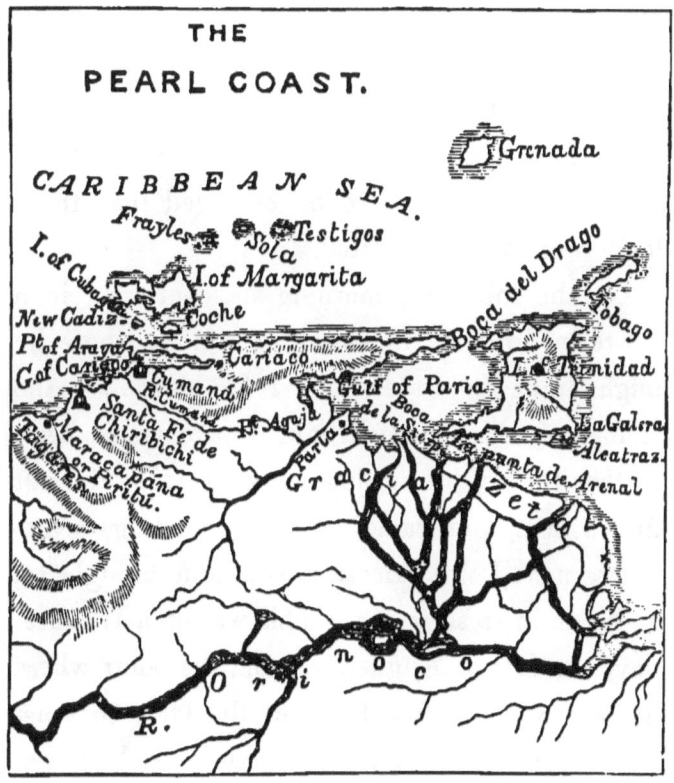

ficiently deep for his vessels to enter, he proceeded westwards.

---

* This point is sometimes placed at the north-east of
Trinidad; but wrongly so. It is now Cape Galeota.—See
HUMBOLT's *Examen Critique*, vol. i. p. 310.

The first thing noticeable as he neared these shores, was that the trees grew well on the margin of the sea. There were houses and people, — and very beautiful lands, which reminded him, from their beauty and their verdure, of the gardens of Valencia as seen in the month of March. It was also to be observed that these lands were well cultivated.

On the following morning he continued in a westerly direction in search of a port, where he might take in water, and refit his ships, the timber of which had shrunk, from extreme heat, so that they sadly needed caulking. He did not find a port, but came to deep soundings somewhere near Point Alcatraz, where he brought to, and took in fresh water. This was on a Wednesday, the first of August. From the point where he now was, the low lands of the Orinoco must have been visible, and Columbus must have beheld the continent of America for the first time.* He supposed it to be an island of about twenty leagues in extent, and he gave it the somewhat insignificant name of Zeta.

---

* The northern part of the continent had been discovered by Sebastian Cabot on the 24th of June, 1497.

The same signs of felicity which greeted his eyes on his first sight of land, continued to manifest themselves. Farms and populous places* were visible above the water as he coasted onwards; with the trees flourishing close to the sea—a sure sign of the general mildness of the weather, wherever it occurs.

The next day he proceeded westwards along the southern part of Trinidad, until he arrived at the westernmost point, which he called "La punta de Arenal;" and now he beheld the gulf of Paria, which he called "La Balena" (the gulf of the whale). It was just after the rainy season, and the great rivers which flow into that gulf were causing its waters to rush with impetuosity out of the two openings† which lead into the open sea. The contest between the fresh water and the salt water produced a ridge of waters, on the top of which the admiral was borne into the gulf at such risk, that, writing afterwards of this event to the Spanish court, he says, "Even to-day

---

* "Vido muchas labranzas por luengo de Costa y muchas Poblaciones."—Las Casas, *Hist. de las Indias*, MS., lib. i. cap. 132.

† The Boca del Drago and the Boca de la Sierpe

I shudder lest the waters should have upset the vessel when they came under its bows."

Previously to entering the gulf, the admiral had sought to make friends with some Indians who approached him in a large canoe, by ordering his men to come upon the poop, and dance to the sound of a tambourine; but this, naturally enough, appears to have been mistaken for a warlike demonstration, and it was answered by a flight of arrows from the Indians.

The admiral, still supposing that he was amongst islands, called the land to the left of him, as he moved up the gulf, the island of Gracia; and he continued to make a similar mistake throughout the whole of his course up the gulf, taking the various projections of the indented coast for islands. Throughout his voyage in the gulf, Columbus met with nothing but friendly treatment from the natives. At last he arrived at a place which the natives told him was called Paria, and where they also informed him that, to the westward, the country was more populous. He took four of these natives, and went onwards, until he came to a point which he named *Punto de Aguja* (Needle Point), where, he says, he found the most beautiful lands in the world, very populous, and whence, to use his own words, "an infinite number of canoes came off to the ships."

Proceeding onwards, the admiral came to a place where the women had pearl bracelets, and, on his enquiring where these came from, they made signs, directing him out of the Gulf of Paria towards the island of Cubagua. Here he sent some of his men on shore, who were very well received and entertained by two of the principal Indians. It is needless to dwell upon this part of the narrative. Very few of the places retain the names which the admiral gave them, and, consequently, it is difficult to trace his progress. He began to conjecture, from the immense amount of fresh water brought down by the rivers into the Gulf of Paria, that the land which he had been calling the island of Gracia was not an island, but a continent, of which fact he afterwards became more convinced. But little time was given him for research of any kind. He was anxious to reach Hispaniola, in order to see after his colonists there, and to bring them the stores which he had in charge; and so, after passing through the "Boca del Drago," and recounoitring the island of Margarita, which he named, he was compelled to go on his way to Hispaniola. We are hardly so much concerned with what the admiral saw and heard, as with what he afterwards thought and reported.   To understand this, it will be desirable to enter somewhat into the scientific questions which occupied the mind of this great mariner and most observant man.

The discovery of the continent of America by Columbus, in his third voyage, was the result of a distinct intention on his part to discover some new land, and cannot be attributed to chance. It would be difficult to define precisely the train of ideas which led Columbus to this discovery. The Portuguese navigations were one compelling cause.   Then the change, already alluded to, which Columbus had noticed in his voyages to the Indies, on passing a line a hundred leagues west of the Azores, was in his mind, as it was in reality, a circumstance of great moment * and significance.

---

* It is the opinion of HUMBOLDT, as mentioned before, that the celebrated division, made by Alexander the Sixth between the Castilian and Portuguese monarchs, was adopted in reference to these phenomena which Columbus had noticed : and, if the line of no variation were a "constant," no better marine boundary could well be suggested.

It was not a change of temperature alone that he noticed, but a change in the heavens, the air, the sea, and the magnetic current.

In the first place, the needles of the compass, instead of north-easting, north-wested at this line; and that remarkable phenomenon occurred just upon the passage of the line, as if, Columbus says, one passed a hill. Then, the sea there was full of sea-weed like small pine-branches, laden with a fruit similar to pistachio nuts. Moreover, on passing this imaginary line, the admiral had invariably found that the temperature became agreeable, and the sea calm. Accordingly, in the course of this voyage, when they were suffering from that great heat which has been mentioned, he determined to take a westerly course, which led, as we have seen, to his discovering the beautiful land of Paria.*

Now Columbus was one of those men of di-

---

* Las Casas, who had other authentic information about this voyage besides the manuscripts of Columbus, says, that the admiral intended to have gone southwards, after he had taken a westerly course, on quitting the place where he was becalmed. Had he done so, which the state of his ships would not permit, he might have been the discoverer of Brazil.

vining minds, who must have general theories on which to thread their observations; and, as few persons have so just a claim to theorize as those who have added largely to the number of ascertained facts (a privilege which they generally make abundant use of), so Columbus may well be listened to, when propounding his explanation of the wonderful change in sea, air, sky, and magnetic current, which he discerned at this distance of a hundred leagues from the Azores.

His theory was, that the earth was not a perfect sphere, but pear-shaped; and he thought that, as he proceeded westwards in this voyage, the sea went gradually rising, and his ships rising too, until they came nearer to the heavens. It is very possible that this theory had been long in his mind, or, at any rate, that he held it before he reached the coast of Paria. When there, new facts struck his mind, and were combined with his theory. He found the temperature much more moderate than might have been expected so near the equinoctial line, far more moderate than on the opposite coast of Africa. In the evenings, indeed, it was necessary for him to wear an outer garment of fur. Then, the natives were lighter coloured, more astute, and braver than those of the islands. Their hair, too, was different.

Then, again, he meditated upon the immense volume of fresh waters which descended into the Gulf of Paria. And, in fine, the conclusion which his pious mind came to, was, that when he reached the land which he called the island of Gracia, he was at the base of the earthly Paradise. He also, upon reflection, concluded that it was a continent which he had discovered, the same continent of the east which he had always been in search of; and that the waters, which we now know to be a branch of the river Orinoco, formed one of the four great rivers which descended from the garden of Paradise.

Very different were the conjectures of the pilots. Some said that they were in the Sea of Spain; others, in that of Scotland, and, being in despair about their whereabouts, they concluded that they had been under the guidance of the Devil. The admiral, however, was not a man to be much in-fluenced by the sayings of the unthoughtful and the unlearned. He fortified himself by references to St. Isidro, Beda, Strabo, St. Ambrose, and Duns

Scotus, and held stoutly to the conclusion that he had discovered the site of the earthly Paradise. It is said, that he exclaimed to his men, that they were in the richest country in the world.

Columbus did not forget to claim, with all due formalities, the possession of this approach to Paradise, for his employers, the Catholic Sovereigns. Accordingly, when at Paria, he had landed and taken possession of the coast in their names, erecting a great cross upon the shore, which, he tells Ferdinand and Isabella, he was in the habit of doing at every headland, the religious aspect of the conquest being one which always had great influence with the admiral, as he believed it to have with the Catholic monarchs. In communicating this discovery, he reminds them how they bade him go on with the enterprise, if he should discover only stones and rocks, and had told him that they counted the cost for nothing, considering that the Faith would be increased, and their dominions widened.

It was, however, no poor discovery of mere "rocks and stones" which the admiral had now made. It will be interesting to see his first impressions of the men and the scenery of this continent which he had now, unconsciously, for the first time, discovered. He says, " I found some lands, the most beautiful in the world, and very populous." The lands in the island of Trinidad he had previously compared to Valencia, in Spain, during the month of March. It is also noticeable that he had observed that the fields were cultivated. Of the people, he says, " They are all of good stature, well made, and of very graceful bearing, with much and smooth hair; " and he mentions that on their heads they wore the beautiful Arab head-dress (called *heffeh*), made of worked and coloured handkerchiefs, which appeared in the distance as if they were silken.

The description given by Columbus of the natives whom he encounters in his voyages is almost always favourable. Indeed, the description of any man or thing depends as much on the person describing, as on the thing or person described. Those little differences in look or dress, which excite the ready mockery of the untravelled rustic, appear very slight indeed to the man who, like Columbus or Las Casas, has seen many lands, and travelled over many minds. The rude Spanish common soldier perceived a far greater difference between himself and the Indian, than did the most accomplished man who visited the Indies, when he made to himself a similar comparison. Occasionally, in a narrow nature, however cultivated, the commonest prejudices hold their ground; but, in general, knowledge sees behind and beyond disgust, and suffices to conquer it.

Columbus, however, found the men, the country, and the products, equally admirable. It is somewhat curious that he does not mention his discovery of pearls to the Catholic monarchs, and he afterwards makes a poor excuse for this. The real reason I conjecture to have been a wish to preserve this knowledge to himself, that the fruits of this enterprise might not be prematurely snatched from him. His shipmates, however, were sure to disperse the intelligence; and the gains to be made on the Pearl Coast were, probably, the most tempting bait for future navigators to follow in the track of Columbus, and complete the discovery of the earthly Paradise.

Of the delights of this Paradise Columbus himself was to have but a slight and mocking foretaste. He had been constantly ill during the voyage, suffering from the gout and from an inflammation in his eyes which rendered him almost blind. His new colony in Hispaniola demanded his attention, and must often have been the cause of anxious thought to him; and the grave but glowing enthusiast made his way to St. Domingo, and afterwards returned to Spain, to be vexed henceforth by those mean miseries and small disputes which afflicted him for the remainder of his days—miseries the more galling, as they were so disproportionately small in comparison with the greatness of such a man, and with the aims and hopes which they effectually hindered.

CHAPTER X.

T was on the 30th of August, 1498, that Columbus arrived at Hispaniola, where he found the state of his colony far from cheering, the defection of Roldan and his followers having put everything into confusion. The admiral supposed at first that the enmity of Roldan's party was chiefly directed against his brother, the Adelantado, and the admiral hoped that, now he had arrived, some agreement would speedily be concluded with Roldan, of which he might inform the catholic sovereigns by the vessels which he purposed to send back immediately to Spain. This was very far, however, from being the case. These vessels, five in number, left the port of St. Domingo bearing no good news of peace and amity amongst the Spaniards, but laden

with many hundreds of Indian slaves, which had
been taken in the following manner. Some cacique failed to perform the personal services imposed upon him and his people, and fled to the
forests; upon which, orders were given to pursue him, and a large number of slaves were captured and put into these ships. Columbus, in his
letters to the sovereigns, enters into an account of
the pecuniary advantage that will arise from these
slave-dealing transactions, and from the sale of
logwood. He estimates, that "in the name of the
sacred Trinity" there may be sent as many slaves
as sale could be found for in Spain, and that the
value of the slaves, for whom there would be a
demand to the number of four thousand, as he
calculated from certain information, and of the
logwood, would amount to forty *cuentos* (*i. e.* forty
million maravedis). The number of slaves who
were sent in these five ships was six hundred, of
which two hundred were given to the masters of
the vessels in payment of freight. In the course
of these letters, throughout which Columbus
speaks after the fashion of a practised slave-
dealer, he alludes to the intended adoption, on
behalf of private individuals, of a system of ex-

change of slaves for goods wanted from the
mother country. The proposed arrangement was
as follows:—The masters of vessels were to
receive slaves from the colonists, were to carry
them to Spain, and to pay for their maintenance
during the voyage; they were then to allow the
colonists so much money, payable at Seville, in
proportion to the number of slaves brought over.
This money they would expend according to the
orders of the colonists, who would thus be able
to obtain such goods as they might stand in need
of. It was upon the same occasion of writing
home to Spain that the admiral strongly urged
upon the Catholic Sovereigns that the Spanish
colonists should be allowed to make use of the
services of the Indians for a year or two until
the colony should be in a settled state, a proposal
which he did not wait for their highnesses' authority to carry out, and which led to a new form
of the *repartimiento*. But this brings us back to
Roldan's story, being closely connected with it.

After great trouble and many attempts at
agreement, in which mention is more than once
made of slaves, the dispute between Roldan's
party, rebels they might almost be called, and

Columbus, was at last, after two years' negotiation, brought to a close. Roldan kept his chiefjusticeship; and his friends received lands and slaves. It brings to mind the conclusion of many a long war in the old world, in which two great powers have been contending against each other, with several small powers on each side, the latter being either ruined in the course of the war, or sacrificed at the end. The admiral gave *repartimientos* to those followers of Roldan who chose to stay in the island, which were constituted in the following manner. The admiral placed under such a cacique so many thousand *matas* (shoots of the cazabi), or, which came to the same thing, so many thousand *montones* (small mounds a foot and a half high, and ten or twelve feet round, on each of which a cazabi shoot was planted); and Columbus then ordered that the cacique or his people should till these lands for whomsoever they were assigned to. The *repartimiento* had now grown to its second state—not lands only, but lands and the tillage of them. We shall yet find that there is a further step in this matter, before the *repartimiento* assumes its utmost development. It seems, too, that in addition to these *repartimientos*,

o

Columbus gave slaves to those partizans of Roldan who stayed in the island. Others of Roldan's followers, fifteen in number, chose to return to Spain; they received a certain number of slaves, some one, some two, some three; and the admiral sent them home in two vessels which left the port of St. Domingo at the beginning of October, 1499.

On the arrival in Spain of these vessels, the Queen was in the highest degree angered by the above proceedings, and said that the admiral had received no authority from her to give her vassals to any one. She accordingly commanded proclamation to be made at Seville, Granada, and other places, that all persons who were in possession of Indians, given to them by the admiral, should, under pain of death, send those Indians back to Hispaniola, " and that particularly they should send back those Indians, and not the others who had been brought before, because she was informed that the others had been taken in just war." The former part of this proclamation has been frequently alluded to, and no doubt it deserves much praise; but from the latter part it is clear that there were some Indians who could justly, according to Queen Isabella, be made slaves. By this time, therefore, at any rate the question had been solved, whether by the learned in the law, theologians and canonists, I know not, but certainly in practice, that the Indians taken in war could be made slaves. The whole of this transaction is very remarkable, and, in some measure, inexplicable, on the facts before us. There is nothing to show that the slaves given to Roldan's followers were made slaves in a different way from those who had been sent over on former occasions, both by the admiral and his brother, for the benefit of the crown. And yet the Queen, whom no one has ever accused of condescending to state craft, seems to deal with this particular case as if it were something quite new. It cannot be said that the crown was favoured, for the question is put upon the legitimacy of the original capture; and to confirm this, there is a letter from the Sovereigns to one of their household, from which it may be inferred, though the wording is rather obscure, that they, too, gave up the slaves which had come over for them on this occasion.

Every body would be sorry to take away any honour from Isabella; and all who are conversant with that period must wish that her proclamation could be proved to have gone to the root of the matter; and that it had forbidden the sending Indians to Spain as slaves, on any pretext whatever.

To return to the affairs of Hispaniola. Columbus had now settled the Roldan revolt and other smaller ones; he had now, too, reduced the Indians into subjection; the mines were prospering; the Indians were to be brought together in populous villages, that so they might better be taught the Christian faith, and serve as vassals to the crown of Castile; the royal revenues (always a matter of much concern to Columbus) would, he thought, in three years amount to sixty millions of reals; and now there was time for him to sit down, and meditate upon the rebuilding of the temple of Jerusalem, or the conversion of Cathay. If there had been any prolonged quiet for him, such great adventures would probably have begun to form the staple of his high thoughts. But he had hardly enjoyed more than a month of repose, when that evil came down upon him, which "poured the juice of aloes into the remaining portion of his life."

The Catholic sovereigns had hitherto, upon the whole, behaved well to Columbus. He had bitter enemies at court. People were for ever suggesting to the monarchs that this foreigner was doing wrong. The admiral's son, Ferdinand, gives a vivid picture of some of the complaints preferred against his father. He says, " When I was at Granada, at the time the most serene Prince Don Miguel died, more than fifty of them (Spaniards who had returned from the Indies), as men without shame, bought a great quantity of grapes, and sat themselves down in the court of the Alhambra, uttering loud cries, saying, that their Highnesses and the admiral made them live in this poor fashion on account of the bad pay they received, with many other dishonest and unseemly things, which they kept repeating. Such was their effrontery that when the Catholic king came forth they all surrounded him, and got him into the midst of them, saying, ' Pay ! pay !' and if by chance I and my brother, who were pages to the most serene Queen, happened to pass where they were, they shouted to the very heavens saying, ' Look at the sons of the admiral of Mosquitoland, of that man who has discovered the lands of deceit and disappointment, a place of sepulchre and wretchedness to Spanish hidalgoes:' adding many other insulting expressions, on which account we excused ourselves from passing by them."

Unjust clamour, like the above, would not alone have turned the hearts of the Catholic sovereigns against Columbus; but this clamour was supported by serious grounds for dissatisfaction in the state and prospects of the colony: and when there is a constant stream of enmity and prejudice against a man, his conduct or his fortune will, some day or other, offer an opportunity for it to rush in upon him. However this may be, soon after the return of the five vessels from St. Domingo, mentioned above, which first told the news of the revolt of Roldan, Ferdinand and Isabella appear to have taken into serious consideration the question of suspending Columbus. He had, himself, in the letters transmitted by these ships, requested that some one might be sent to conduct the affairs of justice in the colony; but if Ferdinand and Isabella began by merely looking out for such an officer, they ended in resolving to send one who should take the civil as well as judicial authority into his own hands. This determination was not, however, acted upon hastily. On the 21st of March, 1499, they authorized Francis de Bobadilla " to ascertain what persons have raised themselves against justice in the island of Hispaniola, and to proceed against them according to law." On the 21st of May, 1499, they conferred upon this officer the government, and signed an order that all arms and fortresses in the Indies should be given up to him. On the 26th of the same month, they gave him the following remarkable letter to Columbus:—

" Don Christopher Columbus, our Admiral of the Ocean: We have commanded the Comñendador Francis de Bobadilla, the bearer of this, that he speak to you on our part some things which he will tell you: we pray you give him faith and credence, and act accordingly.

" I the King, I the Queen.

" By their command,
" MIGUEL PEREZ DE ALMAZAN."

Bobadilla, however, was not sent from Spain until the beginning of July, 1500, and did not make his appearance in Hispaniola till the 23rd of August of the same year. Their Highnesses, therefore, must have taken time before carrying their resolve into execution; and what they meant by it is dubious. Certainly, not that the matter should have been transacted in the coarse way which Bobadilla adopted. It is a great pity, and a sad instance of mistaken judgment, that they fixed upon him for their agent. I imagine him to have been such a man as may often be met with, who, from his narrowness of mind and distinctness of prejudice, is supposed to be high-principled and direct in his dealings; and whose untried reputation has great favour with many people: until, placed in power some day, he shows that to rule well requires other things than one-sidedness in the ruling person; and is fortunate if he does not acquire that part of renown which consists in notoriety, by committing some colossal blunder, henceforth historical from its largeness.

The first thing that Bobadilla did on arriving at St. Domingo was to take possession of the admiral's house (he being at the fort La Concepcion), and then to summon the admiral before him, sending him the royal letter. Neither the admiral nor his brothers attempted to make any resistance; and Bobadilla, with a stupid brutality, which I suppose he took for vigour, put them in chains, and sent them to Spain. There is no doubt that the Castilian population of Hispaniola were rejoiced at Bobadilla's coming, and that they abetted him in his violence. Accusations came thickly against Columbus: " the stones rose up against him and his brothers," says the historian Herrera, emphatically. The people told how he had made them work, even sick men, at his fortresses, at his house, at the mills, and other buildings; how he had starved them; how he had condemned men to be whipped for the slightest causes, as, for instance, for stealing a peck of wheat when they were dying of hunger. Considering the difficulties he had to deal with, and the scarcity of provisions, many of these accusations, if rightly examined, would probably have not merely failed in producing anything against Columbus, but would have developed some proofs of his firmness and sagacity as a governor. Then his accusers went on to other grounds, such as his not having baptized Indians " because he desired slaves rather than Christians:" moreover, that he had entered into war unjustly with the

Indians, and that he had made many slaves, in
order to send them to Castile.   It is highly
unlikely that these latter charges were preferred
by a single colonist, unless, perhaps, by some man
in religious orders.   The probability is, that they
came from the other side of the water; and this
does give considerable strength to the report, that
the displeasure of the court with respect to the
Admiral's proceedings against the Indians had to
do with his removal from the government of the
Indies.   If so, it speaks largely for the continued
admirable intentions of the Spanish court in this
matter.

Poor Columbus!   His chains lay very heavily
upon him. He insisted, however, upon not having
them taken off, unless by royal command, and
would ever keep them by him, ("I always saw them
in his room," says his son Ferdinand), ordering
that they should be buried with him.   He did
not know how many wretched beings would have
to traverse those seas, in bonds much worse than
his, with no room allowed them for writing, as
was his case,—not even for standing upright;
nor did he foresee, I trust, that some of his doings
would further all this coming misery.   In these

chains Columbus is of more interest to us than when in full power as governor of the Indies; for so it is, that the most infelicitous times of a man's life are those which posterity will look to most, and love him most for. This very thought may have comforted him; but happily he had other sources of consolation in the pious aspirations which never deserted him.

We have come now to the end of Columbus's administration of the Indies. Whatever we may think of his general policy, we cannot but regret his removal at the present time, when there appeared some chance of solidity in his government: though we must honestly admit, that the Catholic Sovereigns, with such evidence as they had before them, were far from wrong in recalling him, had it been done in a manner worthy of his and of their greatness.

CHAPTER XI.

THE career of Columbus had already been marked by strong contrasts. First, a " pauper pilot," then the viceroy of a new world; alternately hoping, and fearing, despondent, and triumphant, he had passed through strange vicissitudes of good and evil fortune. But no two events in his life stand out in stronger contrast to each other than his return to Spain after his first voyage, and his return now. He was then a conqueror; he was now a prisoner. He was then the idol of popular favour; he was now the unpopular victim of insidious maligners. In truth, the contrast was so startling as to strike home to the hearts of the common people, even of those—and there were many such—who had lost kinsmen or friends in that fatal quest for gold which the admiral had originated and stimulated.

The broad fact was this: Columbus had given Spain a new world; Spain loaded him with fetters in return. There was a reaction. The current of public opinion began to turn in his favour. The nation became conscious of ingratitude to its benefactor. The nobility were shocked at the insult to one of their own order. And no sooner had the Sovereigns learned from Columbus of his arrival, and of his disgrace, than they issued immediate orders for his liberation, and summoned him to their court at Grenada, forwarding money to enable him to proceed there in a style befitting his rank. They then received him with all possible signs of distinction; repudiated Bobadilla's arbitrary proceedings; and promised the admiral compensation and satisfaction. As a mark of their disapprobation of the way in which Bobadilla had acted under their commission, they pointedly refused to enquire into the charges against Columbus, and dismissed them as not worthy of investigation.

But though the Sovereigns acted thus promptly on the admiral's behalf, there is no doubt that one of them, at least, was in no wise displeased at his being removed from his government. At each fresh discovery, Ferdinand had repented more and more of the concession by which Columbus was to receive an eighth part of the profits of the newly-found countries, and to be their governor-general.   He probably apprehended that this viceroy, when once master of the boundless wealth which was supposed to be nearly within his grasp, would become more powerful than his master, and might finally throw off his allegiance altogether.   But here was an opportunity, without any flagrant breach of faith, of eluding the bargain, by refusing, on very plausible grounds of policy, to reinstate Columbus immediately in his viceroyalty.   Isabella, who had always been his firm friend, would probably have refused to acquiesce in any scheme for absolutely depriving him of his rights, but it was sufficiently obvious that just at present, while the colonists were excited against him, it would be prudent that some one else should take the reins of government.

The Queen granted Columbus a private audience.   He told his story with much simple eloquence—so pathetically, indeed, that his warm-hearted mistress is said to have been moved to tears at the recital.   He described the difficulties which he had encountered and the machinations of the enemies who had been constantly thwarting him. He pleaded that he had been obliged to create a line of conduct for himself, having to deal with an entirely new combination of circumstances without any precedent to guide him. And he implored the Queen to believe that the accusations which had, of late, poured in against him, were prompted by the disappointed ambition and the jealousy of his enemies, and had not any solid foundation in fact.

Isabella replied in a very sensible speech, telling him that, while she fully appreciated his services, and knew the rancour of his enemies, she was afraid that he had given some cause for complaint. "Common report," she said,* "accuses you of acting with a degree of severity quite unsuitable for an infant colony, and likely to excite rebellion there. But the matter as to which I find it hardest to give you my pardon, is your conduct in reducing to slavery a number of Indians who had done nothing to deserve such a fate. This was contrary to my express orders. As your ill fortune willed it, just at the time when I heard of this breach of my instructions, everybody was complaining of

---

* *Charlevoix.*

you, and no one spoke a word in your favour. And I felt obliged to send to the Indies a commissioner to investigate matters, and give me a true report; and, if necessary, to put limits to the authority which you were accused of overstepping. If you were found guilty of the charges, he was to relieve you of the government and to send you to Spain to give an account of your stewardship. This was the extent of his commission. I find that I have made a bad choice in my agent; and I will take care to make an example of Bobadilla, which shall serve as a warning to others not to exceed their powers. I cannot, however, promise to re-instate you at once in your government. People are too much inflamed against you, and must have time to cool. As to your rank of admiral, I never intended to deprive you of it. But you must bide your time and trust in me."

It was arranged that the appointment of the new governor should be for two years only, at the expiration of which period, as Isabella thought, the administration of the colonies might be again entrusted to Columbus; while Ferdinand doubtless considered that some pretext might be found in the meantime for omitting to re-appoint him at all. And though Columbus may have been told verbally that it was their Highnesses' intention to re-instate him after the lapse of two years, it is noteworthy that the document appointing Ovando makes no mention of any limitation of the term of his (Ovando's) government. The words are, "that he is to be governor as long as it is their Highnesses' will and pleasure." Bobadilla, fortunately for the islanders, was forthwith to be superseded; for, if Columbus had chastised them with whips, Bobadilla was chastising them with scorpions. His first object was the discovery of gold; and to secure this he took a census of the natives, and assigned them all as slaves to the colonists. A large proportion of the latter, as we have seen, were simply the scourings of Spanish prisons; and the brutality with which these men treated their wretched helots was very terrible. Some estimate of the amount of pressure employed may be formed from the fact that, although Bobadilla had reduced the royalty payable to the Sovereigns from one-third to one-eleventh of the gold found, this smaller proportion produced a larger revenue. In other words, about four times as much gold was discovered under Bobadilla's system as under that of Columbus.

But when the Sovereigns heard of the cruelties which that system involved, they urged forward the departure of Ovando, whom they had selected as governor, and who, to judge from his previous career, was a man eminently fitted to rule justly and mercifully. He was well known to Ferdinand and Isabella, having been chosen by the Queen as one of the companions for her eldest son, Prince John. With regard to his personal appearance, we are told that he was of moderate stature, and had a " vermilion-coloured beard," which fact hardly conveys much to our minds; but it is added, in general terms, that his presence expressed authority. With respect to his mental qualifications, we learn that he was a friend to justice, an honourable person both in words and deeds, and that he held all avarice and covetousness in much aversion. He was humble, too, they say, and when he was appointed Commendador Mayor of the Order of Alcantara, he would never allow himself to be addressed by the title of " Lordship," which belonged to that office.

Previous to Ovando's departure from court,

the monarchs were particular in giving him instructions both verbal and written. Among these
instructions was one which Isabella especially insisted on, namely, "that all the Indians in Hispaniola should be free from servitude and be un-
molested by any one, and that they should live as
free vassals, governed and protected by justice,
as were the vassals of Castile." Like the vassals
in Spain, the Indians were to pay tribute; they
were also to assist in getting gold, but for this
they were to be paid daily wages. Other com-
mands were given at the same time for the conversion of the Indians, and to insure their being
treated kindly.

Respecting the general government of the
country, it was arranged that on Ovando's going
out, all those who received pay from the government in the Indies, as well those who had accompanied Bobadilla as those who had come out
originally with Columbus, should return to Spain,
and that a new set to replace them should go out
with Ovando. This was done because most
of these soldiers and officials had necessarily been
connected with the late troubles in the colony,
and it would be a good plan to start afresh, as it

were. At the same time it was provided that no
Jews, Moors, or new converts were to go to the
Indies, or be permitted to remain there; but
negro slaves " born in the power of Christians,
were to be allowed to pass to the Indies, and the
officers of the royal revenue were to receive the
money to be paid for their permits." This is the
first notice with respect to negroes going to the
Indies. These instructions were given in the
year 1501.

On Ovando's arrival in the colony, Bobadilla
was to undergo the ordeal of a " *residencia*," a
kind of examination well known and constantly
practised in Spain, to which Authorities were subject on going out of office—being of the nature of
a general impeachment. It is satisfactory to find,
that amongst the orders given to Ovando, there are
some for the restitution of the admiral's property,
and the maintenance of his mercantile rights.

Just before Ovando took leave of the king, he
received a formal lecture upon the duties of a
governor. The King, the Queen, and a privy
councillor, Antonio de Fonseca, were the persons
present; and, as I imagine, the latter addressed
Ovando on the part of their Highnesses. As it is

not often that we have an opportunity of hearing a didactic lecture on the modes and duties of government given in the presence of a great master of that art, and probably looked over, if not prepared, by him, we must enter the royal cabinet, and hear some part of this discourse.

The first point which Fonseca impresses upon Ovando is, that before all things, he is to look to what concerns the reverence of God and His worship. Then he is to examine into the life and capacity of the men about him, and to put good men into office; taking care, however, not to leave all the authority in the hands of subordinates (*here we may well imagine Ferdinand nodded approvingly*), to the diminution of his own power, " nor to make them so great that they shall have occasion to contrive novelties," in order to make themselves greater. Also, let there be change of authorities, so that many may have a share of profit and honour, and be made skilful in affairs.

That he should use moderation in making *repartimientos* and tributes, not overtaxing the people, which moderation would be furthered by his taking care that his personal and his household expenses were within due bounds. (*Here,*

I fancy, the monarchs looked at each other, thought of their own frugal way of living, and Isabella smiled.)

That he should not make himself judge in a cause, but let culprits be tried in the ordinary way.   Thus he will avoid unpopularity, for " the remembrance of the crime perishes: not so that of the punishment." (*This aphorism must, I think, have been composed by Ferdinand himself.   His writing is always exceedingly concise and to the purpose.*)

That he should not listen to tale-bearers, (*parleros*) either of his own household or to those out of it; nor take vengeance upon anybody who had spoken ill of him, it being " an ugly thing to believe that anybody could speak ill of one who did ill to no one, but good to all."   That it is one of the conditions of bad governors, "moved therein by their own consciences" to give heed to what they hear is said of them, and to take ill that, which if it had been said, they had better not have heard.   Rather let injurious sayings be overcome by magnanimity.

That it would be good for him to give free audience to all, and to hear what they had to say; and if their counsel turned out ill, not to look coldly upon them for that. The same in war, or in any other undertaking: his agents must not have to fear punishment for failure, nor calumny for success: " for there were many persons who, to avoid the envy of their superiors, sought rather to lose a victory than to gain it." (*Here Ferdinand ought to have looked a little ashamed, being conscious that his own practice by no means came up to what he perceives to be noble and wise policy in the matter.*)

That he (Ovando) should look to what example he gives both in word and deed,—governors living, as in a theatre, in the midst of the world. If he does ill, even those who follow him in that, will not the less disesteem him.

That although it is necessary for him to know the life of every one, yet he must not be over-inquisitive about it, nor rout up offences which are not brought before him officially. " Since if all offences were looked into, few men, or none, would be without punishment." Besides, for secret faults men may correct themselves: if those faults are made known, and especially if they are punished in excess, shame is lost, and men give way to their bad impulses.

That he is to encourage those who work, and

to discourage the idle, as the universal Father does.

That, as regards liberality, he should so conduct himself, that men should not dare to ask him for things which they would know he must deny: this would be a great restraint upon them, and a great proof of good reputation in a governor.

That, in fine, all that had been said consisted in this, that he was to govern as he would be governed: and that " it behoved him to be intent in business, to show courage in difficulties, and management in all things, brevity in executing useful determinations, yet not as if carried away by passion, but always upon good counsel; considering much what a charge was upon him, for this thought would be useful to him at all times: and above all things he was to take heed (in order that the same thing might not happen to him which had happened to the admiral) that when any occasion for dealing briefly with an offence occurred, he should have swift recourse to punishment, for in such cases the remedy ought to be like a thunderbolt."

After reading the above, we cannot say that

the Catholic monarchs were inattentive to the government of their Indian possessions, nor can the sagacity which directed that attention be for a moment questioned. Indeed that sagacity is so remarkable, that it may naturally occur to the learned reader to inquire, whether Machiavelli's " Prince" had yet been published, and whether King Ferdinand could have read that much-abused manual of crafty statesmen. It was, however, about twelve years after this memorable audience granted by Ferdinand and Isabella to Ovando that " The Prince" is alluded to by Machiavelli, and described as a small unpublished work.

Charged with these instructions, then, Nicholas de Ovando left the port of San Lucas on the 13th of February, 1502, to take possession of his new government, having under him a gallant company of two thousand five hundred persons, a large proportion of them being hidalgoes. On his way he met with a terrible storm, in which one of his largest vessels foundered, and he had some difficulty in reaching St. Domingo at all. This, however, he succeeded in doing on the 15th of April, and entered at once upon the reforms which he was commissioned to institute.

He announced the *residencia* of Bobadilla, and placed Roldan under arrest.   He exerted himself to found settlements along the coast, and at first, no doubt, he endeavoured to carry out the merciful directions which he had received with regard to the Indians.   But, like Bobadilla, he was a knight of a religious order, with a certain narrow way of looking at things incident to his profession, with no especial culture that we know of, and with little originality of character.   In these respects he presented a remarkable contrast to Columbus, who was a man of various accomplishments, large minded, enthusiastic, fluent, affectionate, inventive. And so, whereas Columbus had always treated the natives with consideration and humanity, Ovando soon began to rule them with a rod of iron.   We must not linger too long over his administration of what we may call Columbus's kingdom, but there is one sad episode which it is worth while to recount, if only to make the policy of Columbus stand out in brighter relief.

When Anacaona, the Queen of Xaragua, had received the admiral's brother, Don Bartolomé, on a former occasion, the Spaniards affirmed her to be a wise woman, of good manners, and pleasant address; and she is said to have earnestly entreated her brother to take warning by the fate of her husband, Caonabó, and to love and obey the Christians. As she was now to play the hostess again, this time to Ovando, we may refer to the account of her former reception of a Spanish governor, the Adelantado, of which there are some details furnished by Peter Martyr.

After mentioning that the queen and her brother received the lieutenant with all courtesy and honour, he says: " They brought our men to their common hall, into which they come together as often as they make any notable games or triumphs, as we have said before. Here, after many dancings, singings, maskings, runnings, wrestlings, and other trying of masteries, suddenly there appeared in a large plain near unto the hall, two great armies of men of war, which the king for his pastime had caused to be prepared, as the Spaniards use the play with reeds, which they call *Juga de Canias.* As the armies drew near together, they assailed the one the other as fiercely as if mortal enemies with their banners spread should fight for their goods, their lands, their lives, their liberty, their country, their wives and their children, so that within the moment of an hour, four men were slain, and many wounded. The battle also would have continued longer, if the king had not, at the request of our men, caused them to cease."

At this time, in the year 1503, some of Roldan's former partizans were settled in the province of Xaragua, and were a great trouble to the colony. Herrera says, in a quiet sarcastic way, " they lived in the discipline they had learnt from Roldan ;" and the governing powers of Xaragua found them " intolerable." He also adds that Anacaona's people were in policy, in language, and in other things superior to all the other inhabitants of the island. As might be expected, there were constant disturbances between these Spaniards and the adjacent Indians ; and the Spaniards took care to inform the governor that their adversaries, the Indians of Xaragua, intended to rebel. Perhaps they did so intend. Ovando resolved, after much consultation, to take a journey to Xaragua. It must be said, in justice to Ovando, that this does not look as if he thought the matter were a light one. Xaragua was seventy leagues from St. Domingo. The governor set out well accompanied, with seventy horsemen and three hundred foot-soldiers. Anacaona, who had some suspicion of his intentions, summoned all her feudatories around her " to do honour" to him, when she heard of his coming. She went out to meet Ovando with a concourse of her subjects, and with the same festivities of singing and dancing as in former days she had adopted when she went to receive the Adelantado. Various pleasures and amusements were provided for the strangers, and probably Anacaona thought that she had succeeded in soothing and pleasing this severe-looking governor, as she had done the last. But the former followers of Roldan were about the governor, telling him that there certainly was an insurrection at hand, that if he did not look to it now, and suppress it at once, the revolt would be far more difficult to quell when it did break out. Thus they argued, using all those seemingly wise arguments of wickedness which from time immemorial have originated and perpetuated treachery. Ovando listened to these men; indeed he must have been much inclined to believe them, or he would hardly have come all this way. He was now convinced that an insurrection was intended.

With these thoughts in his mind, he ordered

that, on a certain Sunday, after dinner, all the
cavalry should get to horse, on the pretext of a
tournament.   The infantry, too, he caused to be
ready for action.   He himself, a Tiberius in dis-
sembling, went to play at quoits, and was disturbed by his men coming to him and begging
him to look on at their sports.   The poor Indian
queen hurried with the utmost simplicity into the
snare prepared for her.   She told the governor
that her caciques, too, would like to see this
tournament, upon which, with demonstrations of
pleasure, he bade her come with all her caciques
to his quarters, for he wanted to talk to them,
intimating, as I conjecture, that he would explain
the festivity to them.   Meanwhile, he gave his
cavalry orders to surround the building;   he
placed the infantry at certain commanding posi-
tions;   and told his men, that when, in talking
with the caciques, he should place his hand upon
the badge of knighthood which hung upon his
breast, they should rush in and bind the caciques
and Anacaona.   It fell out as he had planned.
All these deluded Indian chiefs and their queen
were secured.   She alone was led out of Ovando's
quarters, which were then set fire to, and all the

chiefs burnt alive. Anacaona was afterwards hanged and the province was desolated.

Humanity does not gain much, after all, by this man's not taking the title of " Lordship " which he had a right to.

Finally, the governor collected the former followers of Roldan in Xaragua, and formed a town of their settlement, which he named " the city of the true peace " (*La villa de la vera Paz*), but which a modern chronicler well says might more properly have been named " Aceldama, the field of blood." I observe that the arms assigned to this new settlement were a dove with the olive-branch, a rainbow, and a cross.

But it is time to return to Columbus, who in the mean time was chafing at the inactivity which had been forced upon him. His was a restless spirit, perhaps too restless for an organizer, who ought to possess an inexhaustible amount of patience, and to be able to wait as well as to labour. He had formed a theory that some strait existed through which a passage might be made from the neighbourhood of St. Domingo to those regions in Asia from which the Portuguese were just beginning to reap a large profit, and which must be very near that home of the gold which had always occupied his thoughts. He pressed the Sovereigns to provide him with ships for an expedition having for its special object the discovery of this strait; and on the occurrence of some delay as to the equipment of vessels for the purpose, he seems to have written to Ferdinand, reproaching him with the treatment which he had received, and with the want of confidence manifested towards him now. To this Ferdinand answered in a letter which was certainly well calculated to soothe the Admiral's indignation. It was to the following effect, " You ought to be convinced of our displeasure at your captivity, for we lost not a moment in setting you free. Your innocence is well known; you are aware of the consideration and friendship with which we have treated you ; the favours which you have received from us shall not be the last that you will receive; we assure to you your privileges, and are desirous that you and your children may enjoy them. We offer to confirm them to you again, and to put your eldest son in possession of all your offices, whenever you wish. . . . We beg you to set out as soon as possible."

On the 9th of May the preparations were complete, and Columbus set sail from Cadiz with his brother, Don Bartholomew, and his second son, Fernando. As an instance of the admiral's chivalrous love of adventure, it may be mentioned that upon hearing that the Portuguese fortress of Arzilla, on the African coast, was besieged by the Moors, he first proceeded thither, quite voluntarily, to its relief. When he reached it, however, he found that the siege had been raised; and his services were not, therefore, called into requisition.

After a singularly prosperous voyage, he reached Martinique on the 13th of June. His instructions from the Sovereigns expressly interdicted him from visiting St. Domingo; but, on finding that his largest ship required some repairs to make her seaworthy, he boldly disregarded the prohibition, and sent a boat to ask Ovando to furnish him with another vessel in place of the damaged one, and to allow his squadron to take refuge in the harbour during a hurricane which he foresaw to be imminent. Ovando refused both requests. His commission set forth that Columbus was not to visit the island; and the contingency of hurricanes was not provided for. Besides, the governor believed that this prediction of a hurricane was a mere pretext of the admiral's for obtaining admission to the harbour. To an eye unaccustomed to tropical changes, the weather appeared to be " set fair." Scarcely a ripple passed over the sea; scarcely a breath stirred the luxuriant foliage on shore. Ovando repulsed with scorn the admiral's suggestion that, at any rate, the departure of the fleet for Spain should be delayed. This fleet was the richest in cargo that had ever left the islands. It contained all the gold which had been wrung out of the natives by Bobadilla's harsh measures. Of one nugget, especially, the old chroniclers speak in the most glowing terms. According to them, it was the largest piece of virgin gold ever discovered. It had been found accidentally, by an Indian woman at the mines, while listlessly moving her rake to and fro in the water one day during dinner time. Its value was estimated at 1,350,000 maravedis; * and in the festivities which took place on the occasion, it was used as a dish for a roast pig, the miners

---

* Equivalent to about £416.

saying that no king of Castile had ever feasted from a dish of such value. We do not find that the poor Indian woman had any part in the good fortune. Indeed, as Las Casas observes, she was fortunate if she had any portion of the meat, not to speak of the dish. Bobadilla had purchased the nugget for Ferdinand and Isabella, and had shipped it with other treasure valuable enough to go a long way towards compensating the sovereigns for all their expenditure on the new colony—if the fleet could only reach Spain in safety.

But on the second day after its departure the Admiral's prediction became terribly verified. A tornado of unexampled fury swept over the seas; and those on shore could judge of the fate that was likely to befall the unfortunate squadron, as many of the buildings and trees on the island were levelled with the ground by the force of the tempest. Of all the ships, only one—and that the frailest of the fleet—was able to accomplish the voyage to Spain. A few vessels managed to return, in dire distress, to the island; but by far the greater number foundered at sea. The historians of the period do not fail to remark that, while the ship which reached Spain safely was the one carrying the admiral's property, a special providence decreed that his enemies—Bobadilla, Roldan, and their associates in cruelty and plunder—should perish with their ill-gotten gains.

Like Cassandra, Columbus witnessed the discomfiture of the disbelievers in his prophecy: like her he was denied the right of sanctuary upon the occurrence of the disaster which he had foretold. Repulsed from port by Ovando, however, the admiral sailed along the coast, and succeeded in bringing his own ship under the lee of the land when the storm came on. But the three other caravels were in no little danger (particularly the disabled one, which was commanded by the Adelantado), and some days elapsed before the little squadron was re-united in the port of Azua, to the west of San Domingo. Thence he proceeded to Jaquimo, on the extremity of the same coast, and after refitting his ships, set sail for Jamaica on the 14th of July, 1502. Passing that island, he met with light and varying winds, and contrary currents, in the archipelago of reefs and keys which he had previously named the Queen's Garden.

For about nine weeks he made so little progress that his crews began to clamour for the
abandonment of the expedition. The ships were
worm-eaten and leaky. Provisions were running
short. The seamen had seen their commander
thrust away from what might be called his own
door ; and the sight of his powerlessness had
strengthened their independence until it amounted to insubordination. Fortunately, however, before the discontent broke out into open mutiny,
a breeze sprang up from the east, and the admiral
easily persuaded his unruly crews that it was better
to prosecute their voyage than to remain beating
about the islets waiting to return home.

They were soon gladdened by the sight of the
pine-clad slopes of the little island of Guanaja,
lying about forty miles from Truxillo, on the
coast of Honduras. Here there appeared a canoe,
much more like the ships of the old world than
any they had seen before, manned by twenty-five
Indians who had come from the continent on a
trading voyage among the islands. Their cargo
consisted of cotton fabrics, iron-wood swords, flint
knives, copper axe-heads, and a fruit called by
the natives cacao, to which the Spaniards were

now introduced for the first time, but the merits
of which, as a beverage, they were not slow to
appreciate. The admiral treated these people
with much kindness, and won their confidence at
once by presenting them with some of the glittering toys which never failed to dazzle a bar-
barian eye.

One old Indian, whom Columbus selected as
apparently the most intelligent of the band, consented to accompany him as pilot, and indicated,
by signs, his knowledge of a land, not far distant,
where there were ships, and arms, and merchandize,
and, in fact, all the marks of civilization which
were displayed to him by the Spaniards themselves, and with which he professed to be per-
fectly familiar. Whether he intended to mislead
Columbus, or whether, like most of his race, he
was merely proud of being impassive, and of
being able to repress all indication of astonish-
ment at startling novelties, it is certain that his
demeanour and his signs were interpreted by the
admiral to indicate an acquaintance with a country, rich and civilized, lying towards the east;
which country could, of course, be no other than
the long sought-for kingdom of the Grand Khan.

Had Columbus, in pursuance of his first intention,
steered to the west, a few hours would have
brought him to the coast of Yucatan; and the
riches of Mexico would have rewarded his discovery. But this savage, like his evil destiny,
crossed his path at the critical moment, and turned
him from the road to fortune.

Steering along the coast of Honduras, on the
12th of September, he reached Cape Gracias a
Dios, to which he gave this name in pious thank-
fulness for the southerly turn taken by the land
at that point, so that the east winds, which had
hitherto obstructed him, were now favourable to
his course along the coast. A month later he
entered several bays on the Isthmus of Panama,
where he was able to procure provisions and to
refit his vessels, but failed to obtain any intelligence either of the kingdom of the Khan, or
of the strait which he fancied would lead him
there. The natives whom he encountered were
generally disposed to be friendly; but, in one
instance, when the depth of water in a creek
obliged him to moor his vessels close to the shore,
an attack of the Indians was only repulsed by the
use of artillery, the thunder and lightning of which

seemed always to possess, in the eyes of the savages, a supernatural and therefore awful character. On another occasion, when a conference was held with one of the tribes, great alarm was caused by a notary, who attended to take notes of the conversation. The savages had never before seen the operation of writing; and they regarded it as a spell which was to have some magic effect upon them, and which they must neutralize by various mystic fumigations which they believed to act as counter-charms. " They were themselves skilled sorcerers," says Columbus,—whose credulity in such matters was only that of his age.

It was not until the 5th of December that the admiral could resolve to abandon his easterly course, although the conviction had been gradually forcing itself upon him that the condition of his ships was such as to render a prosecution of his voyage almost impossible. He had scarcely turned back, intending to found a settlement on the river Veragua, before he encountered a storm which tried his worm-eaten caravels very severely. The thunder and lightning were incessant; the waterspouts (the first they had seen) threatened to engulph them; huge crests of waves burst in phosphorescent floods over them; and their escape, if we consider the smallness of the caravels, and the force of a tropical cyclone, was little less than miraculous. At last, after eight days' tossing to and fro, the admiral gained the mouth of a river, which he named the Bethlehem, because he entered it on the day of the Epiphany.

In this neighbourhood there was a powerful cacique, named Quibia, whose territory contained much gold, and with whom, therefore, the Spaniards were anxious to treat. But he outwitted them. Offering to supply them with guides to conduct them to his gold mines, he really sent them, not to his own mines, but to those of a rival cacique, of Urira. Here, however, they succeeded in acquiring, by barter and by actual discovery, large quantities of the precious metal, which seemed to be so abundant, that the admiral made sure that he had come to the very Aurea Chersonesus from which Solomon had obtained the gold for the temple at Jerusalem. He had seen more signs of gold here in two days, he said, than he had seen in St. Domingo in four years. His first step was to form a settlement to provide a depôt for the gold which might be collected. A convenient site was found near the mouth of the river Bethlehem, and by the end of March the Adelantado had built a village of huts, in which it was proposed that he should remain, with about eighty followers, while Columbus returned to Spain for supplies.

But rumours soon reached the Adelantado of a projected attack on the settlement by the natives, and he took measures to seize Quibia in his own palace. The Indians, dismayed at the capture of their cacique, offered large quantities of gold for his ransom, but the Adelantado preferred to keep him as a hostage for peace. However, as he was being conveyed down the river, on board one of the boats, he managed, although bound hand and foot, and in the custody of one of the most powerful of the Spaniards, to spring over-board and to make his escape, swimming under water to the shore. Henceforward, as might have been expected, there was war to the knife between the natives and the settlers. An attempt was made to burn down the village by means of blazing arrows. A boat's crew of eleven Spaniards, who had proceeded some distance up the river, were attacked by savages in canoes, and only one man escaped to carry to the settlement the news of the massacre of his companions.

The admiral, with three of the caravels, was in the offing, awaiting a wind favourable for his departure, but the dry weather had made the river so shallow that it was impossible for the caravel left with the settlers to cross the bar, and as they had no boat strong enough to weather the surf, it seemed impossible for them to carry to him tidings of their condition. They were in despair; for if they were left, they knew that they were left to perish. The admiral, on his part, had become uneasy, not knowing that their failure to communicate with him was owing to the fact that their only seaworthy boat had been destroyed by the Indians. His own boats were small and scarcely weathertight. But some of Quibia's family who had been taken on board the squadron as prisoners, had made their escape by swimming to the shore, three miles off; and this feat encouraged a bold pilot of Seville, named Ledesma, who was on board the admiral's caravel, to attempt a similar exploit. Never was bearer of reprieve for the condemned more welcome.

Ledesma communicated with the Adelantado, and conveyed to the admiral intelligence of the desperate state of affairs. The result was, that when in a few days the wind moderated, all the settlers were taken on board the squadron, which now only consisted of three ships, as it was found necessary to abandon the caravel which had been left inside the harbour bar.

And there was no time to spare. The rough weather had severely tried the crazy and worm-eaten vessels; and anxiety and want of rest were having their effect on Columbus. Making his way first to Porto Bello, where he was obliged to leave another caravel as no longer seaworthy, on the 31st of May he quitted the coast at a point on the west of the Gulf of Darien, and steered northward towards Cuba. A collision between his two remaining ships rendered them still more unfit to cope with the squalls and breakers of the Archipelago; but at last, in the middle of June, with his crews in despair, nearly all his anchors lost, and his vessels worm-eaten so as to be " as full of holes as a honey-comb," he arrived off the southern coast of Cuba, where he obtained supplies of cassava bread from friendly natives.

CHAPTER XII.

AILING to make head against the wind so as to reach Hispaniola, Columbus shaped his course for Jamaica, and there, in the harbour which he had named Santa Gloria on his former visit, his voyage was perforce brought to a conclusion. As his ships could not float any longer, he ran them on shore, side by side, and built huts upon the decks for housing the crews. Such a habitation, like the Swiss lake dwellings, afforded remarkable advantages of position in case of attack by a hostile tribe.

The admiral's first care was to prevent any offence being given to the aborigines which might give cause for such an attack. Knowing, by sad experience, the results of permitting free intercourse between the Spaniards and the natives, he enforced strictly a rule forbidding any Spaniard to go ashore without leave ; and took measures for regulating the traffic for food so as to prevent the occurrence of any quarrel.   Diego Mendez, who had been his lieutenant, and had shown himself the boldest of his officers throughout this voyage, volunteered to proceed into the interior of the island to make arrangements for the periodical supply of provisions from some of the more remote tribes, as it was certain that the sudden addition to the population would soon exhaust the resources of the immediate neighbourhood.   This service Mendez performed with great adroitness, and a regular market was established to which the natives brought fish, game and cassava bread, in exchange for Spanish toys and ornaments.

Although the Spaniards were thus secure from starvation for the present, their position was most critical.   The journey to the easternmost extremity of Jamaica would probably not be unattended with difficulty and danger, for it must be effected through the midst of Indian tribes, hostile to each other, and therefore probably not unanimous in being friendly towards strangers.   But the most formidable obstacle to communication with the government of Hispaniola was the strait of forty leagues' breadth, full of tumbling breakers and rushing currents, which separated the two islands. However, it was necessary that the attempt should be made; and Diego Mendez, though he considered it to be "not merely difficult, but impossible, to cross in so small a vessel as a canoe," volunteered for the service, after all the other Spaniards had declined to undertake it. He was to be the bearer of a letter from the admiral to Ovando, asking him to send a vessel to release the castaways from their imprisonment, and of a despatch to the Sovereigns, giving a detailed account of the Admiral's voyage and a glowing description of the riches of Veragua. This despatch is very characteristic of the writer, bearing, as it does, the marks of strong enthusiasm, of almost fanatical superstition, of confidence in the midst of despair, and of exultation in the face of ruin. Describing his reflections during the storm at the mouth of the river Bethlehem, he breaks into the following rhapsody, which, probably in perfect good faith, dwells on the contrast between the goodness of God and the bad faith of man, in a way which ought to have touched Ferdinand nearly. It is worth quoting at full length, as an example of the wild fervour of a rapt enthusiast.

"Wearied and sighing," writes Columbus, "I

fell into a slumber, when I heard a piteous voice
saying to me, 'O fool, and slow to believe and
serve thy God, who is the God of all! What did
He more for Moses, or for His servant David,
than He has done for thee? From the time of
thy birth He has ever had thee under His peculiar care. When He saw thee of a fitting age,
He made thy name to resound marvellously
throughout the earth, and thou wert obeyed in
many lands, and didst acquire honourable fame
among Christians. Of the gates of the ocean sea,
shut up with such mighty chains, He delivered to
thee the keys; the Indies, those wealthy regions
of the world, He gave thee for thine own, and
empowered thee to dispose of them to others,
according to thy pleasure. What did He more for
the great people of Israel, when He led them forth
from Egypt? Or for David, whom, from being a
shepherd, He made a king in Judæa? Turn to
Him, then, and acknowledge thine error: His
mercy is infinite. He has many and vast inherit-
ances yet in reserve. Fear not to seek them.
Thine age shall be no impediment to any great
undertaking. Abraham was above a hundred
years when he begat Isaac; and was Sarah

youthful? Thou urgest despondingly for succour. Answer! Who hath afflicted thee so
much, and so many times, God, or the world?
The privileges and promises which God hath
made to thee He hath never broken,* neither hath
He said, after having received thy services, that
His meaning was different, and to be understood
in a different sense. He fulfils all that He promises, and with increase. Such is His custom.
I have shown thee what thy Creator hath done
for thee, and what He doeth for all. The present
is the reward of the toils and perils thou hast
endured in serving others.' I heard this," adds
Columbus, " as one almost dead, and had no
power to reply to words so true, excepting to
weep for my errors. Whoever it was that spoke
to me finished by saying, ' Fear not! All these
tribulations are written in marble, and not without cause.' "

" Though this be madness, there is method in
it;" but still, the whole character of Columbus
forbids us to assume that this alleged vision was
merely an ingenious device for remonstrating with

---

* A sarcasm to " catch the conscience of the king."

R

the Sovereigns. It must not be forgotten that in those times the popular belief as to such matters was very different from that which obtains now; and that Columbus was as credulous as his cotemporaries on the subject of the supernatural. It was easy for an imagination like his to be wrought upon so as to give to " airy nothings," to the " thousand phantasies that crowd into the memory," the character of special revelations from heaven. In this very despatch his religious fervour is displayed again and again. Jerusalem, according to the prophecy, was to be rebuilt by the hand of a Christian. He would be that Christian. Prester John, so said tradition, had asked for missionaries to instruct him in the true faith. He would conduct them to the kingdom of this unknown potentate. Then he goes on to deplore his own hard case; " surrounded by cruel and hostile savages; isolated, infirm, expecting each day will be my last; severed from the holy sacraments of the Church, so that my soul, if parted here from my body, must be for ever forgotten. . . . . . If it should please God to deliver me hence, I humbly supplicate your majesties to permit me to repair to Rome, and

perform other pilgrimages." Columbus, then, being really convinced of the fatal consequences of
not being within reach of formal communion with
the Church, must have felt that he was risking
more than his mere bodily life when he wandered into those unknown countries; that he
staked both body and soul on his success.

Laden with these despatches, Mendez and a
Spanish comrade set out along the coast in a
canoe manned by six Indians. The party arrived
safely at the easternmost Cape of Jamaica (now
called Point Morant); but while awaiting calm
weather for crossing the strait to Hispaniola,
they were attacked by a tribe of savages, who
overpowered them by sheer force of numbers,
and carried them off as captives. The beads and
toys, however, which Mendez had taken with
him to barter with the natives, were too attrac-
tive not to claim the chief share of the attention
of his conquerors; and while they were settling
the division of the spoil he managed to effect his
escape to his canoe, and to return in it in safety
to Santa Gloria. As soon as a second canoe could
be procured, Mendez was ready to make a second
attempt, but on this occasion he stipulated that he

should be accompanied to the easternmost point of Jamaica by a force sufficient to protect him from the hostile tribes.   Accordingly, on the 7th July, 1503, the Adelantado, with an armed escort, proceeded along the shore; while Mendez, with six Spaniards and ten Indians, in one canoe, and Fieschi (a Genoese, who had commanded one of the caravels), with a like number in the other, made their way by sea to Point Morant.

After waiting a short time for fine weather, the two canoes started for Hispaniola, and reached a little island called Navazza on the third day, both Spaniards and Indians having suffered terribly from the want of water, with which they were insufficiently supplied.   Another day's labour at the oar brought them to Cape Tiburon, where Mendez left his companions and proceeded alone to St. Domingo.   Here he was informed that the governor had left for Xaragua; and thither he made his way alone, through fifty leagues of wild forest country, to represent to Ovando the necessity of sending relief to the admiral, and that speedily.   Ovando seems to have temporized.   He dreaded the return of Columbus, as likely to excite the seditious to a revolt against his own government. And so far from taking active steps in the matter himself, it was only with reluctance that he authorized Mendez to proceed to St. Domingo to purchase a caravel on behalf of Columbus, in which Fieschi might return to Santa Gloria, and bring him off.

Meanwhile, month after month passed by, and the unfortunate castaways at Santa Gloria had no tidings from Hispaniola, and were even ignorant whether their messengers had succeeded in reaching that island. At last, in January, 1504, the murmurs against the inaction of Columbus broke out into open mutiny. Francesco Porras, the captain of one of the caravels, headed the mutineers, and going to the admiral, who was confined to his bed by the gout, told him that he, the admiral, evidently was afraid to return to Spain; but that the people had determined to remain no longer to perish, and intended to depart at once. On this there arose shouts from the followers of Porras, " To Castile! We follow!" The admiral made a temperate speech, pointing out the danger of attempting to leave the island in mere canoes, and the absurdity of supposing that he had not a common interest with them in all respects. But

Porras was as persistent in his desire to go, as Columbus in his determination to stay; and, taking possession of the canoes which had been purchased from the natives, the mutineers set out on their journey towards Hispaniola, leaving the admiral and his brother with scarcely any adherents except those whom sickness incapacitated for undertaking the journey.

The progress of Porras and his followers through the island was marked by a series of outrages on the natives which completely neutralized the effect of the admiral's conciliatory policy. They seized forcibly on whatever provisions could be found, and mockingly referred the owners to Columbus for payment. Three attempts to cross over to Hispaniola failed in consequence of rough weather. On one occasion the canoes were in so much danger of being swamped that the Spaniards cast everything on board into the sea; and, as this did not lighten the canoes sufficiently, they then proceeded to force overboard their unfortunate companions, the Indians, who swam after them for a long time, but sank one by one, being prevented by the swords of the Spaniards from approaching. Abandoning, as hopeless, their design of reaching Hispaniola, the mutineers then proceeded to roam over the island, quartering themselves on the Indians, and committing every possible excess.

Of course the influence of this conduct on the relations between Columbus and the natives, was soon apparent. The trinkets and beads, which had once been so precious in their eyes, had first lost the charm of novelty, then the value of rarity. The circulating medium became so depreciated that provisions were scarcely procurable. And, similarly, the personal veneration which the natives had first evinced for the white men, had given way to contempt and to hatred, when familiarity had shown how worthless were these " superior beings." The Indians refused to minister to their wants any longer; and famine was imminent.

But just at this last extremity, the admiral, ever fertile in devices, bethought him of an expedient for re-establishing his influence over the Indians. His astronomical knowledge told him that on a certain night an eclipse of the moon would take place. One would think that people living in the open air must be accustomed to see such eclipses sufficiently often, not to be particularly astonished at them. But Columbus judged—and as the event proved, judged rightly—that by predicting the eclipse he would gain a reputation as a prophet, and command the respect and the obedience due to a person invested with supernatural powers. He assembled the caciques of the neighbouring tribes. Then, by means of an interpreter, he reproached them with refusing to continue to supply provisions to the Spaniards. "The God who protects me," he said, "will punish you. You know what has happened to those of my followers who have rebelled against me; and the dangers which they encountered in their attempt to cross to Haiti; while those who went at my command,* made the passage without difficulty. Soon, too, shall the divine vengeance fall on you; this very night shall the moon change her colour and lose her light, in testimony of the evils which shall be sent upon you from the skies."

The night was fine: the moon shone down in full brilliancy. But, at the appointed time, the

---

* This was a gratuitous assumption: as the admiral had as yet no tidings of the success of Mendez.

predicted phenomenon took place, and the wild howls of the savages proclaimed their abject terror. They came in a body to Columbus, and implored his intercession. They promised to let him want for nothing if only he would avert this judgment: as an earnest of their sincerity they collected hastily a quantity of food, and offered it at his feet. At first, diplomatically hesitating, Columbus presently affected to be softened by their entreaties. He consented to intercede for them; and, retiring to his cabin, performed, as they supposed, some mystic rite which should deliver them from the threatened punishment. Soon the terrible shadow passed away from the face of the moon; and the gratitude of the savages was as deep as their previous terror. But, being blended with much awe, it was not so evanescent as gratitude often is; and henceforward there was no failure in the regular supply of provisions to the castaways.

Eight months had passed away without any tidings of Mendez, when, one evening there hove in sight a small caravel which stood in towards the harbour of Santa Gloria, and anchored just outside. A boat which put off from the caravel brought on shore her commander, a certain Diego de Escobar, whom Columbus recognized as a person whom he had sentenced to be hanged as a ringleader in Roldan's mutiny, and who had been pardoned by Bobadilla. The proceedings of this person—whose reprieve must have now seemed to the admiral particularly injudicious—were singular enough. Standing at a distance from Columbus, as if the admiral had been in quarantine, he shouted, at the top of his voice, a message from Ovando, to the effect that he (the governor) regretted the admiral's misfortunes very keenly, that he hoped before long to send a ship of sufficient size to take him off. He added, that in the meantime, Ovando begged him to accept a slight mark of his friendship. The "slight mark of his friendship" was—a side of bacon, which, with a small cask of wine and a letter from Ovando, he delivered to the admiral: and rowed off as fast as possible. The whole scheme of this visit, which was probably planned by Ovando with the object of ascertaining the real condition and designs of Columbus, was in the last degree insulting to him and tantalizing to his companions, with whom D'Escobar would not permit any communication to be held. However, the admiral wrote a civil reply to Ovando, describing piteously the hardships of his condition, and disclaiming any ulterior design with regard to the government of Hispaniola. Carrying this missive, D'Escobar set sail at once, and was out of sight, on his return voyage, before the morning of the day after his arrival.

This mysterious visit was by no means satisfactory to the admiral's companions. As he alone had held communication with D'Escobar, he was free to give them whatever account he chose of his interview; and this liberty, it may be parenthetically observed, he did not scruple to exercise somewhat at the expense of strict truth. He represented himself as having refused to depart with D'Escobar, because the caravel was too small to carry them all away, and he was determined to share their lot, confident in Ovando's assurance of speedy succour. He made overtures for a reconciliation to Porras, and endeavoured to persuade the mutineers to return on board the ships. But these overtures were scornfully repulsed and the admiral's messengers were sent back with threats of force. As for the caravel, Porras had

little difficulty in persuading his credulous followers that it was merely an apparition which
Columbus had conjured up by magic arts; and
such was the reputation for sorcery which the
admiral had acquired by his astronomical observations, that even the sight and taste of some tan-
gible bacon (half of that present from Ovando of
which we have heard) which he sent as a peace-
offering to the mutineers, failed to convince them
of the material character of the supposed phantom
ship.

Soon, however, the differences between the
rival parties were brought to an issue.   The
Adelantado received information that Porras was
planning a descent on the ships, with the object
of seizing the stores and capturing the admiral.
Resolving to anticipate this attack, he placed himself at the head of fifty* devoted partisans of
Columbus, and sallied out to engage the mutineers.   A furious struggle ensued; but the Ade-

---

* It would appear from this number that either there
had been some defection from the ranks of the mutineers,
or that more than half the Spaniards had remained faithful
to the admiral.

lantado performed prodigies of valour, and his
followers were better supplied with fire-arms than
the rebels; so that the latter sustained a complete
defeat, and their leader Porras was carried off as
a prisoner to the ships.

The natives, who had been spectators of the
affray, were much perplexed. Wiser people than
these poor savages have looked with sorrowful
wonder on the appeal to brute force to decide the
quarrels of nations; and the Indians, when they
saw strife and death among the beings whom they
had formerly considered as heaven-descended and
immortal, felt that their estimate of these attri-
butes ought to be lowered. But when curiosity
impelled them to examine the corpses of the
Spaniards who had been killed in the encounter,
after minutely inspecting several bodies, they
came to that of Ledesma—whose name may
be remembered as that of the gigantic pilot of
Seville who swam through the surf at Bethlehem
to the Adelantado's relief—who had now fallen,
covered with wounds, fighting on behalf of the
mutineers. As the savages proceeded to thrust
their fingers into his wounds, Ledesma, who had
fainted from pain, recovered consciousness, and

uttered a stentorian yell which put the Indians to flight, says an ancient chronicler, "as if all the dead men were at their heels." And as Ledesma eventually recovered, notwithstanding his having received wounds sufficient to kill three ordinary persons, the natives must have been inspired by a proper respect for the almost miraculous vitality of the white men.

The victory gained by the Adelantado was conclusive. The rebels at once submitted to the admiral, who consented to pardon them; reserving only their ringleader, Porras, for future punishment. It was arranged that they should not again take up their habitation on board the ships, but Columbus sent ashore a trusty lieutenant as their commander, and supplied them at the same time with European articles to barter for food with the natives. And so the two bands of castaways —one on ship and one on shore—awaited the promised succour, with the weariness of hope deferred.

CHAPTER XIII

T was not till the 28th of June, 1504, when just a year had elapsed since their arrival at Santa Gloria, that the Spaniards were gladdened by the sight of the two caravels which had been sent—one by Mendez, the other by Ovando—to their relief. Their embarkation, as may be supposed, was quickly effected; but adverse winds made the voyage to Hispaniola a long one, and the two vessels did not reach St. Domingo before the 13th of August.

Much to the surprise of the admiral, he found himself treated with the most punctilious courtesy by Ovando, who even proceeded to the harbour, with a numerous suite, to receive him in state upon his arrival. However, differences soon arose as to the conflicting jurisdictions of the viceroy and the governor; especially with regard to the case of Porras, whom Ovando, in opposition to the admiral's wish, insisted upon releasing from custody. Moreover he even announced his intention of instituting a general enquiry as to the events which had taken place in Jamaica, in order to decide whether Porras and his associates had been justified in their rebellion. Columbus disputed the right of Ovando to take upon himself the office of judge in such a matter; and remarked that his own authority as viceroy must have sunk very low indeed, if it did not empower him to punish his officers for mutinying against himself. This dispute was unfortunate as regards the private interests of the admiral, for the revenues arising from his property in the island had been collected under the authority of the governor, who, upon the occurrence of this quarrel, was easily able to raise difficulties in the way of his obtaining a fair account of the proceeds. But he was all the more anxious to return to Spain; and, within a month from his arrival at St. Domingo, he started homeward in the caravel which had brought him from Jamaica.

But even in this last voyage he was forced to " make head against a sea of troubles." His evil star was in the ascendant. Twice his vessel nearly foundered. Twice her masts were sprung in successive tempests. His own health was succumbing to the acute attacks of gout which had become more and more frequent for the last few years. And so, prostrated by sickness, nearly ruined in means, and now hopeless of encouragement from the Sovereigns, the discoverer of the New World arrived at Seville, on the 7th of November, 1504, in as miserable a plight as his worst enemy could have wished.

He could scarcely expect to be received with much favour at court. He had failed in the search for that strait leading to the kingdom of the Grand Khan, the discovery of which had been the special object of his expedition; he had lost his ships; he had brought home wonderful stories of golden lands, but no gold. Porras* was at large,

---

* It seems just possible that, as the original narrative of the mutiny of Porras was written by Fernando Columbus, who would naturally take his father's side, something is to be said for Porras which has not been said for him by historians

and had influence at court, which enabled him to
stimulate the existing prejudice against Columbus.

Poor, old, infirm, he had now to receive intelligence which was to deepen all his evils. He
remained at Seville, too unwell to make a journey
himself, but sent his son Diego to court, to manage
his affairs for him. The complaints of the admiral,
that he had no news from court, are quite touching. He says, he desires to hear news each hour.
Couriers are arriving every day, but none for him:
his very hair stands on end to hear things so contrary to what his soul desires. He alludes, I imagine, to the state of the Queen's health; for, in a
memorandum of instructions to his son, written at
this period, the first thing, he says, to be done is,
" to commend affectionately, with much devotion,"
the soul of the Queen to God. Could the poor
Indians but have known what a friend to them
was dying, one continued wail would have gone
up to heaven from Hispaniola and all the western
islands. The dread decree, however, had gone
forth, and on the 26th of November, 1504, it was
only a prayer for the departed that could have
been addressed; for the great Queen was no
more. If it be permitted to departing spirits to

see those places on earth they yearn much after, we might imagine that the soul of Isabella would give " one longing, lingering look" to the far West.

And if so, what did she see there? How different was the aspect of things from what governors and officers of all kinds had told her: how different from aught that she had thought of, or commanded! She had insisted that the Indians were to be free: she would have seen their condition to be that of slaves. She had declared that they were to have spiritual instruction: she would have seen them less instructed than the dogs. She had ordered that they should receive payment for their labour: she would have found that all they received was a mockery of wages, just enough to purchase once, perhaps, in the course of the year, some childish trifles from Castile. She had always directed that they should have kind treatment and proper maintenance: she would have seen them literally watching under the tables of their masters, to catch the crumbs which fell there. She would have beheld the Indian labouring at the mine under cruel buffetings, his family neglected, perishing, or enslaved. She would have marked him on his return, after eight months of dire toil, enter a place which knew him not, or a household that could only sorrow over the gaunt creature who had returned to them, and mingle their sorrows with his; or, still more sad, she would have seen Indians who had been brought from far distant homes, linger at the mines, too hopeless, or too careless, to return.

Turning from what might have been seen by Queen Isabella, had her departing gaze pierced to the outskirts of her dominions, we have to record the closing scene of the strange eventful history of Columbus, who did not long survive his benefactress. Ever since his return from his fourth voyage to the Indies, he had done little else than memorialize, and petition, and negotiate about his rights. But Ferdinand, who had always looked coldly on his projects, was disposed to regard his claims with still less favour. Columbus professed himself willing to sacrifice the arrears of revenue due to him, but urged strenuously his demand that his son Diego should be made viceroy of the Indies, in accordance with the terms of the grant making that dignity hereditary in his family. Ferdinand did not refuse absolutely: the breach of faith would have been too flagrant. But he procrastinated, and ended by referring the matter to the significantly named Board of Discharges of the Royal Conscience, which board regulated its proceedings by the known wishes of the king, and procrastinated too.

The proverb, " Fear old age, for it does not come alone," was especially applicable to Columbus, while suffering sickness without the elasticity to bear it, poverty with high station and debt, and all the delay of suitorship, not at the beginning, but at the close, of a career. A similar decline of fortune is to be seen in the lives of many men.; of those, too, who have been most adventurous and successful in their prime. Their fortunes grow old and feeble with themselves; and those clouds, which were but white and scattered during the vigour of the day, sink down together, stormful and massive, in huge black lines, across the setting sun.

Shortly after the arrival of Philip and his queen in Spain, Columbus had written to their Highnesses, deploring his inability to come to them, through illness, and saying that, notwithstanding his pitiless disease (the gout), he could yet do them service the like of which had not been seen. Perhaps he meant service in the way of good advice touching the administration of the Indies ; perhaps, for he was of an indomitable spirit, that he could yet make more voyages of discovery. But there was then only left for him that voyage in which the peasant who has seen but the little district round his home, and the great travellers in thought and deed, are alike to find themselves upon the unknown waters of further life. Looked at in this way, what a great discoverer each of us is to be! But we must not linger too long, even at the deathbed of a hero. Having received all the sacraments of the Church, and uttering as his last words, " *In manus tuas, Domine, commendo spiritum meum*," Columbus died, at Valladolid, on Ascension Day, the 20th of May, 1506. His remains were carried to Seville and buried in the monastery of Las Cuevas ; afterwards they were removed to the cathedral at St. Domingo ; and, in modern times, were taken to the cathedral at Havana, where they now rest.

THE END.

www.ingramcontent.com/pod-product-compliance
Lightning Source LLC
Chambersburg PA
CBHW020340030726
47496CB00007B/1953